STEALING JOSH

ESPECIALLY FOR GIRLS® Presents

STEALING JOSH

THE PORTRAITS COLLECTION™

Susan Blake

FAWCETT GIRLS ONLY • NEW YORK

This book is a presentation of **Especially for Girls®**, Newfield Publications, Inc. Newfield Publications offers book clubs for children from preschool through high school. For further information write to: **Newfield Publications, Inc.,** 4343 Equity Drive, Columbus, Ohio 43228.

Edited for Newfield Publications and published by arrangement with Ballantine Books, a division of Random House, Inc. Especially for Girls and Newfield Publications are trademarks of Newfield Publications, Inc.

RL   VL 6 & up
          ————————
          IL 8 & up

A Fawcett Girls only Book
Published by Ballantine Books

Library of Congress Catalog Card Number: 90-93054

ISBN 0-449-14606-5

Manufactured in the United States of America

First Edition: August 1990

1

"**M**AY I SHOW YOU TO YOUR SEAT, MISS MICHAELS?"

The young man who held out his arm was wearing a gray tuxedo with a small yellow rose in the lapel. He gestured up the church aisle toward the row where I was supposed to sit, in front of my cousin Annie and her mother, my aunt Ruth. My seat was marked with a big white bow, so that everybody who came to the wedding would know I was a special guest. Since I was sitting on the right side, they would also know that I belonged to the groom's party.

Of course nobody had to be told that I was the groom's daughter. Even though my dad and I had only arrived the week before, Vermilion, Illinois, was a small town, and all 4,449 residents probably already knew every detail about us. After all, my father had lived here from the day he was born until he went away to college, then moved to Washington, D.C. Everybody was probably twittering over the fact that he had rediscovered his high

1

school sweetheart in a chance meeting in Washington, fallen in love all over again, and decided to move back with his daughter, get remarried, and set up a new medical practice. In Vermilion what else was there to talk about except other people's business? Life here was probably one big soap opera.

"*May* I, Miss Michaels?" Gray Tux repeated insistently, raising his voice over the organ music. His annoyed tone made it clear that I was holding up the parade, but I wasn't exactly anxious to take my place in front of that white bow. Reluctantly I took his arm and let him escort me down the aisle, past Annie, who gave me a thumbs-up sign and winked.

"Way to go, Lauren," she whispered as the usher bowed and I took my seat.

Actually this *wasn't* the way to go as far as I was concerned. It seemed dumb to make such a big deal out of the wedding. What did I need to be here for anyway? It didn't have anything to do with me. I felt like stamping on Gray Tux's shiny black shoe, thumbing my nose at everybody, running out the door, and going back to D.C. It gave me a wicked pleasure to imagine the raised eyebrows and the gasps of startled surprise that would come if I actually *did* leave.

But of course I couldn't do that. Dad and Carolyn had been upset enough when I'd refused to be Carolyn's maid of honor. My skipping out on their wedding would probably be grounds for divorce— my father's divorcing *me*, that is. So, here I was, wearing a stupid, ruffly, yellow dress—Carolyn's idea, naturally—and a floppy-brimmed straw hat and ridiculous white gloves, also Carolyn's idea, trying to look demure and happy, as if I approved of what my father was doing.

Soon after I was settled in my seat, a door to the right of the altar opened, and the minister came out, followed by my father and his best man, Uncle Paul, who was Annie's father. They stood in front of the bank of roses that decorated the altar—roses we had spent all morning gathering from Carolyn's garden. Dad looked very handsome, even distinguished, in his dark gray tuxedo. He had a striped tie, and a boutonniere of lily of the valley was tucked in his lapel.

A lump formed in my throat when I saw that. Lily of the valley had always been my mother's favorite flower. I wondered if Dad remembered that. I wondered how Mom would feel today if she were still alive. She might be happy for him, I thought, trying to swallow the lump. She had always believed in people having what they wanted. Well, I wasn't my mom. I didn't want him to have what he wanted, if what he wanted was a new wife. Maybe that wasn't fair, but it was the way I felt.

With a flourish the organist broke into the first thundering chords of "Here Comes the Bride." Everybody turned expectantly. It was time for Carolyn's grand entrance.

I couldn't see her yet, but the flower girl had started down the aisle. It was Carolyn's ten-year-old daughter, Maggie—a pain in the neck, in my opinion. Maggie hadn't wanted to be in the wedding, either. I knew for a fact that she felt pretty much the same as I did about the idea of her mom and my dad getting married, even though she probably had different reasons. But since she was only ten, she couldn't do much about it. So, here she was, marching down the aisle with a sullen expression on her face, looking like a skinny doll in her ruffled yellow dress (a smaller version of mine), and her floppy-brimmed hat and white gloves. Her blond hair was pulled back with combs, and to complete the charming picture, there was a big fat wad of bubble gum in her cheek.

There was a rustle as Carolyn's sister appeared, wearing a deep yellow gown, and behind her, Carolyn herself on her brother's arm. The organ music swelled as she walked down the aisle. Even I had to admit that she looked very pretty, her straight blond hair loose and flowing under her ivory veil. Carolyn was thin and wiry, almost like a boy; the lines of her lace-trimmed ivory dress made her look more feminine than usual. With her arms full of yellow roses and her face shining with happiness, she looked much younger than forty-one. I guess that's what love does to you. It makes you beautiful.

But not as beautiful as Mom, I thought. In a weird, selfish way, I had become glad that Mom had died so quickly. Her brain tumor had neither disfigured her nor made her linger, terminally ill, for months or years. For her it had been fast and painless. My own pain would be with me for a long time. I turned around stiffly to face the altar. As Carolyn took her place beside my father, the lump came back into my throat. No way was she as beautiful, as feminine, as—

I made myself stop. It wasn't fair to compare them. But I *couldn't* not compare them. My mom had been tall, with gray eyes and long, curly, dark brown hair—like me—and she'd had a beautiful willowy figure. She'd loved dressing up for an evening at the symphony or the opera, to be followed by dinner at a fancy restaurant.

Carolyn was cute, but I never thought of her as beautiful. She dressed simply in jeans and T-shirts. She owned her own nursery, called FlowerFields, and her nails were always grubby from digging in the dirt. It was a good thing she didn't love the symphony and the opera and fancy restaurants, I figured, because there weren't any in Vermilion. But she did like cookouts, and apparently everyone else around here did, too; half the town had come to the one we'd had the night before. She also liked square dancing and bike riding and family picnics at the lake—none of which were my idea of fun.

Back home my friends and I went sailing on the Potomac. Sometimes we'd go to the museums, or go make faces at the baboons in the zoo, or check out the clothes in Georgetown. Before Carolyn, my dad and I used to have dinner at least once a month at our favorite little French restaurant. For the past year, while she and Dad had been dating long-distance, I had tried to get used to the idea of sharing him. But no one ever said it was going to be easy.

The minister looked out into the congregation.

"If anyone knows any reason why these two should not be joined together in marriage," he said, "speak now, or forever hold your peace."

I clenched my hands together. Something inside me wanted to stand up and shout "No!" But that was childish nonsense. Dad had made his choice, even if I couldn't understand how he could love Carolyn after he'd loved my mother. I frowned. The truth was, he'd loved Carolyn *before* he loved my mother, and that was what hurt. They'd been high school sweethearts. But then Dad had gone away to college and met my mother. After that he'd forgotten all about Carolyn.

The minister raised his hand. "Samuel Eugene Michaels, do you take this woman . . ."

Or maybe he hadn't, I told myself fiercely. Maybe, even while he was married to Mom, he had secretly wished he'd married Carolyn instead. But I didn't want to think that. I didn't want to imagine my father being disloyal to my mother, even in his thoughts. It was an *awful* thought.

The minister turned to Carolyn. "Carolyn Joyce Masterson, do you take this man . . ."

With a sigh I began to count all the other things I'd had to give up in the move to Vermilion: our terrific apartment with its view of the Potomac; the great high school I'd gone to; a whole group of friends I'd known practically since birth; and Rich, the guy I'd been dating for four months. I sighed again. I had given up everything, and for what? For my father's romance, that's for what. For a small town stuck in the middle of a big cornfield.

For a dinky high school. For a bratty little stepsister—

The minister raised his hands and said, "You may kiss the bride."

The church was silent, as my father lifted Carolyn's veil. I could see the happiness in their faces; it was like a circle around the two of them, shutting everyone out, shutting *me* out.

Suddenly a loud noise echoed through the church, startling Dad and Carolyn out of their kiss.

Pop!

It was Maggie's bubble gum.

2

"**I** CAN'T BELIEVE SHE DID THAT," ANNIE SAID AS I followed her up the stairs to her room. She ran a hand through her short hair. "How embarrassing!"

The wedding and reception had finally ended, and I'd come back to Annie's with her and Aunt Ruth and Uncle Paul. I was staying with them until Dad and Carolyn got back from their honeymoon.

"I believe it," I retorted grimly. "It's the kind of thing Maggie's been doing ever since my dad and I got to Vermilion. She's always got to be the center of attention." I dumped my bags on the floor of Annie's bedroom and flung myself on one of the twin beds. "But Maggie's the least of my troubles," I said wearily. "If it weren't for you, Annie, I'd probably hurl myself off a bridge."

"There aren't any bridges in Vermilion," Annie replied. "The tallest thing we've got is a two-story building." She gave me an impish grin. "Of course we could always drive to Springfield, and you could jump off the top of the state capitol. That would

8

make you the center of everybody's attention—for a while, anyway."

I smiled. That was the Annie I remembered, always full of wild, crazy ideas. I never knew what kind of trouble she'd get us into—like the time she bet me we could drive the Hensons' tractor around their cornfield without their ever finding out. We were only eleven; we didn't even have permits, much less our licenses! I don't remember what kind of excuse she made up when Mr. Henson found us up on the seat, trying to figure out how to start the thing, but whatever it was, he'd let us off the hook. And another time, when Annie was on some Mata Hari spying kick, we sneaked out of the house late one night to spy on a boy who lived down the street from her. Now that I think of it, we couldn't exactly have been subtle—wearing dark glasses and hats and running to hide behind telephone poles. When we tried to sneak back into the house, her parents were waiting for us. If it had been my dad, we would definitely have been grounded, but Annie found a way to get us out of trouble. Her schemes were always a little hair-raising, but I wouldn't have missed them for anything.

"What did you bring to wear?" Annie asked. She had opened my suitcase and was rummaging through it. "Did you bring that green top I used to like so much?"

I sat up. "Annie, that was *five* summers ago. We were twelve. I threw that shirt out years ago."

"Too bad." She pulled out a bright strawberry-colored blouse. "Hey, this is okay."

"Not with your hair, it isn't," I said. Annie is one

of the prettiest girls I know, but strawberry definitely isn't her color. Most reds just clash with her
short coppery hair, bright green eyes, and creamy
pale skin.

Annie squinted at me. "Speaking of hair, are you
sure you're not dying yours? It looks different."

"Only my hairdresser knows for sure," I said jokingly, lifting my hair with my hands.

I folded my hands behind my head with a smile
and leaned back against the pillow. *This* was more
like it. This was like the old times, the summers
that Annie and I had spent together, back in the
years before Mom died. Every summer my parents
would take a month-long trip somewhere, and I'd
go to Vermilion to stay with Aunt Ruth and Uncle
Paul and Annie.

I'd always had a wonderful time. Annie and I did
nothing but talk. We'd lie on quilts on the lawn
and talk, watching the white fluffy clouds floating
across the Illinois sky. We'd bike to the lake and
talk, eating peanut-butter sandwiches and slapping
mosquitoes. We'd sit on her bed and talk late into
the night, keeping our voices low so that nobody
would hear us. We talked about boys and clothes
and love. We talked about getting our periods and
having babies when we grew up. There were never
any secrets between us. We weren't just cousins,
we were best friends.

After I went back to Washington, we wrote long
letters. Annie's were on pastel paper, and I kept
them in a drawer stuffed with all my favorite sou-
venirs and mementos. I still had those letters, al-

though now they were in a box in the back of my closet.

They told a lot about Annie. It wasn't that she wrote big essays on her philosophy of life or anything. But the way she wrote about dances and hayrides and the other things she did with the kids in Vermilion, I could tell she was popular. And then, when she started dating, she wrote me all about the guys she had crushes on, and I could picture her falling in and out of love with the same quick energy she did everything else. Maybe she was a little unsophisticated and didn't have a lot of experience, but she was open and unpretentious, and I loved her for that.

"Do you still make funny circles over your *is*?" I asked.

Annie laughed. She stopped rummaging in my suitcase and lay down on the other twin bed. "I gave that up last year," she said. "It looked juvenile."

"Now that you're all grown up, I see you're into computers," I joked, glancing at the fancy computer on her desk.

"Yeah, I'm planning to major in computer science in college next year," she said. "I talked to one of the professors at the University of Illinois, and he says it's a great field to go into. I've already got my first-semester courses picked out."

I stared at her. Things *had* changed. The Annie I remembered suffered from math anxiety and had trouble planning her evening. Suddenly she had half her life planned out. Now that she mentioned it, I remembered her writing something about computers in one of her letters, but I guess a part of me still remembered her the way she was when we were younger. "What happened to being a glamorous model?" I asked with mock seriousness.

"That was juvenile, too," she said with a grin.

Five years ago, the summer Mom died, Annie had been walking around with a book balanced on her head, practicing posture, and reading *Vogue* and *Seventeen*. That was the year I wanted to be a flight attendant and fly all over the world for free. But after that, Dad didn't take any more long trips, and I didn't spend summers in Illinois.

Annie and I kept on writing, though, and our letters became more and more important to us. You can say things in letters sometimes that you can't say in person. A lot of the time we would write about ordinary stuff, like which rock group we liked, and how school was going. But we also shared how we felt about growing up; about the right and the wrong way to kiss a boy; how far to go with somebody; the way our bodies were developing. I could tell her when I was scared or uncertain and know she would understand. Even though we hadn't seen each other for five years, I never stopped considering Annie my best friend. And I knew she felt the same way. Friends for life, we always said. I meant it, and I knew Annie meant it, too.

I'd been dying to spend some time with her, but until today, getting ready for the wedding had taken up almost every hour. Now we had a whole week together before Dad and Carolyn got back from their honeymoon, before Maggie got back from her grandmother's.

"Okay," I said. "So, here I am, dying to catch up. Tell me everything. Tell me about your computer. Tell me about your sex life. Tell me about"—I took a deep breath—"Vermilion High. And don't stop talking until you hear me snore."

"Okay," Annie agreed happily. "I'll start with Josh. He's the most important thing."

"Josh." I frowned. "Didn't you write to me about somebody named Larry?"

"Where have you *been*?" Annie demanded. "That was last year, and anyway, he wasn't important. Josh and I just started dating in June." The way Annie's big green eyes were glistening, I could tell she was crazy about the guy. "His name is Josh Reynolds. He took me to the Spring Ball. Oh, Lauren, he's absolutely incredible. And the really wild thing is that I'm the first girl he's ever been serious about. I mean, he's always been kind of a loner, you know, keeping to himself. He never dated very much, even though all the girls are crazy about him because he's so cute."

I felt a stab of envy. Annie looked as starry-eyed about this guy Josh as Carolyn did about my father, and I immediately felt closed out, the way I'd felt at the wedding. It seemed as if the whole world was a couple. Everybody but me. I'd never been in love. I was one of those people who didn't believe in love at first sight. What counted wasn't chemistry, it was personality and intelligence and niceness, and you couldn't judge those things at one glance. So, when all my friends were falling in love with a new guy every week, I was waiting for the real thing.

In the meantime, there was Rich. He'd been my boyfriend during my junior year. But the emphasis was definitely on *friend*, and our romance had never really got heavy, the way some other kids' had. Still, saying good-bye to him hadn't been easy. Frowning, I pushed the recollection of Rich out of my head. I wasn't going to spoil a perfectly good week with Annie by feeling sorry for myself for getting a raw deal. Or by envying her because she'd found the real thing.

Annie reached behind her and handed me a framed photo. "This is Josh."

The guy in the snapshot was leaning against the wing of a small airplane. His hands were casually stuffed into his pockets, his dark hair was falling into his eyes, and there was a lazy half-smile on his face. My eyes widened, and I could see immediately why Annie had fallen for him. He was incredibly handsome. And not only that, there was a certain self-assurance about him, too. Not cockiness, exactly, but he definitely looked like a guy who had everything under control. As I looked at the photo, a warm feeling swept over me, and for a moment it seemed as though he were smiling out of the photo directly into my eyes.

"Wow!" I said, handing it back to her. "He's cute. Does he actually fly that airplane, or is it just for decoration?"

Annie put the photo carefully back on her bedside table. "Josh has his private pilot's license," she said proudly. "He's taken me up a couple of times.

He and his dad are away at some flying meet, but when he gets back, I'm sure he'll be glad to take you for a ride, too."

"Sounds good," I said a little doubtfully. It would be just like Annie to take off in a small plane at the drop of a hat, but the idea made me nervous. I'd flown a number of times, but only in big jets, and I wasn't exactly sure I wanted to go flying around in that dinky little plane. Giving the photo one more glance, I turned back to Annie and changed the subject.

"Besides flying," I asked, "what other fabulous entertainment do you have planned? An exotic afternoon with the computer? Shopping at Neiman-Marcus? A midnight supper at some gourmet restaurant, after a fun evening at the ballet? I brought a long, sexy, black dress and my three-inch heels and pearls, just in case."

Annie gave me a look. "Oh, we'll do better than *that*," she said airily. "If you want to go shopping, we can always go to Andrews Quality Clothing on the square. They have the latest in plaid blouses. Or we can phone in an order out of the Sears catalog if you'd rather."

I laughed.

"And if it's midnight suppers you're after," Annie continued, "maybe you'd settle for a ham sandwich and some lemonade out on the porch swing— if the mosquitoes aren't too bad, that is. And I don't think you'll need your black dress or your pearls," she added, "unless you want to wear them to the Sweet Corn Festival and the county fair. And to the lake, of course."

"Awesome," I muttered.

Annie shook Baxter at me. Baxter was this battered-looking stuffed bear she'd had since we were kids. "Don't put on your big-city act with me, Lauren Michaels."

I raised my chin. "I'll put on my big-city act with you any day I please, Annie Michaels. Just you wait until you see me in my black dress—*ow!*" I yelled, trying to twist away as she pummeled me with Baxter. Then she began tickling me. "Oh, don't! Please don't! I can't stand it!" I screeched, breathless from laughing.

What happened next was the kind of thing that used to happen a lot when we were eleven. Annie tickled me on the sides, and I tickled her on the feet, and in a minute both of us were giggling hysterically, like a couple of little kids.

"Oh, Lauren," Annie said, catching her breath. "I've missed you. I'm so glad you're here. It's better than having a best friend. It's like having a *sister*."

"I don't think I could stand it in Vermilion without you," I said honestly.

Annie took a tissue and handed me one. "Listen, Vermilion isn't so bad," she said. "I'll introduce you to all the guys—"

"All three of them?"

Annie grinned. "I'm sure you'll fall in love with at least two of them. Oh, Lauren, I can't wait to introduce you to Josh. He's so wonderful. I hate to sound like a broken record; it's just that . . . well, he's really *exciting*, if you know what I mean."

"I hope this wonderful guy has a wonderful

friend," I said. "I wouldn't mind some excitement myself."

A knock sounded at the bedroom door, and Aunt Ruth opened it. "Are you girls ready for supper?" she asked. "The fried chicken's on the table."

"And potato salad?" I asked.

"And lemon meringue pie," Aunt Ruth added.

"Ah," I said. "I knew there had to be a reason for coming to Vermilion."

Summer in Illinois. Summer in corn country.

It was the second week in August, and there wasn't a cloud in the sky. I could see the heat rising in shimmery waves out of the green cornfields that stretched toward the horizon in all directions. I could see it on the asphalt road, like puddles of translucent silver that evaporated as we drove toward them and reappeared like shiny ripples in the distance. I could see it on the farmers' dusty, sunburned faces and hear it in their voices when they said, "Warm today, ain't it?" I could taste it in the sharp, salty, tang of sweat on my tongue. Every morning the sun rose like a hot orange ball, and every night it set in a canopy of hot pink and purple.

Even the nights were sweltering. Back in Washington the summers were pretty hot, too, but our apartment there had been air-conditioned, so it was easy to sleep. Here my flimsy nightgown clung to my perspiring body as I tossed restlessly in the twin bed across the room from Annie. I listened to her quiet, even, breathing, I envied her dreams of Josh—dreams that were probably sweet, since she usually smiled in her sleep. In Washington, the streetlight outside my window lit the sidewalks and the tops of cars; the hum of late-night traffic filled the air. Here, the moonlit night was heavy and rich with the fragrance of the creamy honeysuckle that climbed the wall under the window, and all I could hear was the sad, lonely, singing of a single whip-poorwill.

Sometimes I didn't fall asleep until well after midnight, my damp nightgown wound about my legs. No wonder, after such nights, I slept late in the cooler mornings, and only wakened when I heard the cheerful clattering of pots and pans and the rich smells of Aunt Ruth's hearty breakfasts of bacon, eggs, and biscuits.

The days were a little better. After breakfast Annie and I would get dressed and walk the three blocks to the dime store. We always went to the cosmetics counter to buy a lipstick, some nail polish, or perfume. And if we had the change, we would make a brief stop at the local drug store. It was the old-fashioned kind, with a polished wood soda fountain, and we'd drink iced lemonade or soda. Sometimes we'd stroll past the courthouse in the middle of the square, where old men with canes sat napping on benches in the shade of the huge maples. Then we'd saunter home again, to mow the lawn or help Aunt Ruth pick beans and tomatoes in the garden. It wasn't my idea of a thrilling time, but it was so nice to see Annie that at least I never got bored. And anyway, it was too hot to do much else.

Most afternoons we drove Annie's old red Volkswagen to the Lake Vermilion Sportsman's Club and lay on the sandy beach. While we sipped iced tea out of a thermos and covered ourselves with suntan lotion, we'd watch the little sailboats skimming the blue water and gossip about any good-looking guys who zipped past on their water skis. That was when I started to get an idea of what Vermilion High would be like. Annie told me how much fun we'd be having, going to football games and pep rallies together, shopping and double-dating. I was curious, but none of it sounded very exciting to me. Still, when I told Annie all about Franklin High, I tried not to show how much I missed it. I didn't want to sound like a snob. After all, I was going to be spending my entire senior year here. Annie talked a lot about Josh, too. I told her about Rich, but there wasn't really much to say, and before long Annie was plotting ways for me to meet guys here in Vermilion.

One night, halfway through the week, we went to the fairgrounds. It was nearly dusk when we arrived, and the lights made the place look unreal and magical. While we stuffed ourselves on cotton candy, popcorn, and corn dogs, we wandered through the grounds. Apart from the rides, there were food and crafts displays and competitions in everything from canned preserves to quilting. At the baked goods table I wasn't surprised to see that Aunt Ruth's chocolate cake had won a blue ribbon.

After a while we decided to go to the barns. They smelled awful, but Annie didn't seem to mind, so I didn't say anything. I noticed right away that there were a lot of guys, and I looked sideways at Annie and smiled—knowing Annie, I knew that was the reason we'd come here. We ran into a boy Annie knew named David Maloney. He was good-looking with sun-bleached hair and muscular, very tanned arms. David showed us his heifer, a pretty brown-and-white calf named Lucy. We spent the next twenty minutes following David through the maze of pens. He showed us the other calves, horses, chickens, and pigs, and was nice about pointing out the different breeds and explaining what the judges looked for. I was amazed. It was the first time I'd seen so many live animals, outside of the National Zoo. David had a soft, rolling voice and an unhurried way of talking that was nice to listen to. He really seemed to know what he was talking about, and he was easy and comfortable with the animals. I found myself stealing sideways glances at him, admiring his tanned arms and the way he handled Lucy. Not that I'm a great animal lover—the kids in Washington would have thought it was hilarious if they saw me with all those barn animals—but I had to respect the special way he treated them.

Annie nudged me and whispered that I should try to get to know David better. I sidled nervously around a huge brown horse with enormous hooves that looked as if it would kick out at me any second. I wasn't sure what to do. David seemed okay, and he was cute, too, but I wasn't sure how I felt about going out with a guy whose idea of fun was hanging out in a livestock barn.

When we'd finished our grand tour, David turned to us. "Hey," he said, "want to go for a ride on the

Ferris wheel?" He asked both of us, but his eyes were on me.

"I'd love to," Annie said, "but I can't. I'm afraid of heights."

I turned to her, surprised. "Since when?" I asked. "I've been with you on a Ferris wheel before."

Annie elbowed me sharply. "It just started recently."

I shut up. If Annie wanted me to go on the Ferris wheel alone with David, who was I to complain? We left her and climbed on.

We swung up into the velvety sky. The stars above us sparkled like diamonds, and the lights of the midway threaded below like shiny beads. All around I could hear the sweet-sad carnival music, and the shouts of the vendors below.

The wheel turned quickly, and we spun around and around, with the warm breeze in our faces. Then we stopped, suspended at the top, our seats rocking gently, the world spread out under our feet.

David's arm was across the back of my seat. "Having fun?" he asked.

"Yes," I said, and I meant it. Vermilion wasn't Washington, but at that moment, I thought, *There are things here I like, people I like, too, and maybe David could be one of them*.

"I'll be gone for the next couple of weeks," David said. "My folks and I are driving out to the Rockies for vacation. When I get back, school will be starting." His voice was soft and steady as he went on, "Maybe we could go out together then. What do you think?"

"I'd like that," I answered. "I'd like that very much."

David leaned forward, his eyes on mine. "Good," he said. Then he kissed me—not a deep, passionate, kiss, but a soft, gentle, one. "I have the feeling that we're going to be seeing a lot of each other."

It wasn't exactly an original remark, but David seemed like . . . well, like a nice guy. I hadn't fallen head over heels in love with him, but under the magical spell of the sparkling lights and the carnival music, I could almost believe he was right.

3

DAD AND CAROLYN CAME BACK FROM THEIR HONEY-moon late Friday night, bringing Maggie with them. They'd picked her up in Springfield, where she'd stayed with her grandmother. I had already gone to bed by the time they arrived. When I came down to breakfast the next morning, the first thing I saw was Dad and Carolyn kissing. They were being pretty passionate and not bothering to hide it, either. I stood in the doorway clearing my throat and shifting uncomfortably from one foot to the other. I couldn't decide whether to watch or look away.

When they finally saw me, they weren't even embarrassed. Dad just dropped his arms and said, "Good morning, honey," in a cheerful voice. Carolyn smiled and turned to put a pot of blooming chrysanthemums on the table. "Good morning, Lauren," she said. "How would you like your eggs this morning?"

I cleared my throat, feeling even more embar-

rassed because they obviously *weren't* embarrassed. "Scrambled," I muttered.

When Maggie came down to breakfast, I could
tell that the attitude I'd seen at the wedding hadn't
changed a bit, even though she'd had a week to
get used to the idea that we were supposed to be
one big, happy, family. She started off with a surly
grunt in reply to Dad's pleasant, "Would you like
some orange juice, Maggie?" and things went
downhill from there. Inside three minutes she'd
managed to spill her orange juice into her scrambled eggs and drop her toast on the floor, jelly side
down. But Dad and Carolyn kept acting cheerful
and happy, as if nothing were the matter.

"How would you like to go shopping for school
clothes today, Lauren?" Carolyn asked when she'd
finished cleaning up Maggie's mess.

I didn't know what to say. I could imagine the
kind of shopping we'd be doing at Andrews Quality
Clothing. If I bought a blouse there, I could bet that
half the girls at Vermilion High would have one
exactly like it. And the idea of shopping for clothes
with Carolyn wasn't exactly thrilling, either. I had
always loved buying clothes with my mother; she'd
had a wonderful fashion sense and always seemed
to find the perfect things. I was pretty sure that
Carolyn didn't have the same instinct.

"I was thinking," Carolyn went on, not noticing
my hesitation, "that we might drive over to Ur-
bana. The University of Illinois is there, and I'm
sure you'll be able to find a store you like."

"I want to go," Maggie put in quickly. "I need
new school clothes, too."

It was obvious that Maggie just wanted to butt in on our shopping trip. If it had been me, I would have told her that she was acting like a four-year-old, but Carolyn just put her hand on Maggie's arm and gave her a comforting smile.

"I planned for you and me to go another time, honey, just the two of us. That way, we'll have the whole day to ourselves." That was obviously what she'd planned for me, too. A cozy day for a new mother to get acquainted with her new daughter.

"That's okay, Carolyn," I said quickly. "Why don't you take Maggie today? Annie and I already have plans for this afternoon."

There was a hurt look in Carolyn's eyes. My dad started to say something, but she shook her head at him slightly, and he stopped. When she replied, her tone was warm and cordial.

"Of course, Lauren," she said. "You and Annie go ahead and have a good time."

Maggie shot me a triumphant look. "And *we* can go shopping today, can't we, Mom? Can we have lunch at that place I like? And go to the park, too?"

"Sure thing," Carolyn said.

Suddenly I felt torn. Carolyn had wanted this to be an expedition for the two of us, and I'd turned her down. It was a jerky thing to do, but I wasn't sure I wanted to act like a daughter—Carolyn's daughter. Beside me Maggie was jiggling her foot against my chair in an annoying way, and I gritted my teeth as I ate my scrambled eggs. I was *absolutely* sure I didn't want to act like a sister.

* * *

"Annie, that light was almost red!" I cried. "Would you please slow down?"

Josh was back from the airplane meet, and Annie and I had decided to go out to the airport that afternoon to see him. We were both dressed casually in tank tops and shorts, but Annie had spent a lot of time fixing her hair and putting on her makeup. I could tell how excited and happy she was about seeing Josh, and I couldn't help envying her just a little.

"He's been gone for three whole weeks," she said, when I mentioned that she seemed just a little overexcited. She'd just run another yellow light, at Howard Road and Third Street. "Wouldn't you be excited if you hadn't seen the guy you loved desperately for three entire weeks?"

I gave a small laugh. "How am I supposed to know? I've never loved anybody desperately. Or even semi-desperately, for that matter."

Annie gave me an understanding look. "Well, maybe that will change when David gets back," she said. She braked suddenly to avoid hitting a little old lady in an ancient Chevy who was pulling out of the supermarket parking lot, and I jerked forward.

"I wish you'd pay more attention to your driving and stop trying to manage my love life," I told her, pretending to be cross.

Annie giggled. "Somebody's got to manage it. Just wait. I have the feeling that you and David are about to have a wonderful romance, and my feelings are never wrong."

I covered my eyes with my hands to keep from

seeing the speedometer. "Then maybe you'd better make an extra effort," I said, "to keep me alive until he gets back!"

The Vermilion County Airport was about seven or eight miles south of town, in the middle of an immense bean field. A long, low, concrete building was marked Terminal. That was a laugh. It certainly didn't look anything like the airport terminals I'd seen at Washington National. It consisted of a long lobby with a counter at one end. There was one door at the back and another behind the counter that looked like it led to storage for air freight. That was it. The lobby was empty except for a balding, heavyset man behind the counter, who was eating a piece of fried chicken.

"You lookin' for Josh?" he asked Annie in a nasal twang. Without waiting for an answer, the man pointed out the big glass window behind him. "He was out at the hangar, last I saw."

"Thanks, Jumbo," Annie told him, then motioned to me. "This way."

We went out the back door and across a concrete apron shimmering in the heat. A dozen small airplanes were moored to the concrete with heavy chains.

"That's Josh's plane," Annie said, pointing at a white one, with a wide blue stripe down the side and the letters N22127 on it.

I eyed the plane doubtfully. N22127 looked awfully small, nothing like the Boeing 727s I'd been on. I was beginning to reconsider my agreement to go flying. Maybe the two of them could go, and I could watch from the ground.

Off to the right, across the concrete, I could see three big metal buildings with sliding doors, big enough to drive an airplane into.

"Hangars," Annie said, with an explanatory gesture. "Josh's dad owns a couple of airplanes. He takes people up for rides and aerial photography—stuff like that. Josh will, too, when he gets his commercial license. He already does a lot of maintenance on their planes," she added proudly. "And he knows everything there is to know about them." She gave me a half-shy, half-embarrassed glance. "I guess maybe I talk too much about him, huh?"

I smiled and shook my head. Maybe it did get a little old, listening to her go on and on about Josh. But I was happy that Annie was so in love, and I was prepared to like Josh, no matter what, because *she* cared about him, and I cared about her.

We came around the corner of a hangar, and there he was. I recognized him right away from the picture. He was sitting cross-legged on the concrete, wearing a pair of ragged denim cutoffs, a dirty red T-shirt, and oil-stained sneakers. He had a wrench in one hand and a screwdriver in the other, and he was utterly absorbed in his work.

I stopped in my tracks, feeling self-conscious and prickly. I could feel my face getting hot, and suddenly I wished I'd worn something else, something a little more flattering, even though I knew that was crazy.

Annie had paused, too, a little in front of me. "Hi," she said breathlessly.

Josh looked up, pushing aside a shock of dark hair. He had dark eyebrows and the bluest eyes

I'd ever seen. There was a smear of oil on his cheek above the dark shadow where he probably hadn't shaved that day.

"Well, *hi*," he said. He jumped up, dropping his wrench, and held out his arms to Annie, who was already running toward him. He swung her in a circle and kissed her. For the second time that day I didn't know whether to watch or look away.

Josh solved the problem by pulling back. With his arms still around Annie's shoulders, he stepped toward me.

"You must be the famous cousin," he said, smiling. The corners of his eyes crinkled, and his teeth were white against his tanned face. "Welcome to Vermilion."

I just stared at him dumbly for a second. "Hi, Josh," I finally said, croaking the words out.

His dark blue eyes held mine for an electric moment, and I felt breathless, as if he'd been whirling *me* around in his arms. There was . . . I don't know, an odd tension in the moment.

"Are you going to take us for a ride today?" Annie asked, interrupting with a tug at his arm. "I told Lauren you would."

Josh was still looking at me, almost as if he hadn't heard Annie. Then he shook his head and shot a quick grin at me. "Have you ever been in a small plane, Lauren?"

"Just big jets," I admitted.

"Well, then, let's go take a look at the Cessna," he said. "When you've ridden a lot of airliners, a sports plane can look kind of flimsy. I wouldn't blame you for having second thoughts about going up. If you feel uncomfortable about it, all you have to do is so say so."

I gave him a grateful glance. He'd read my mind.

"But maybe you won't feel that way when you've had a closer look at the plane." He led the way around the hangar to the white plane Annie had pointed out to me.

"Do you like to fly?" I asked, then immediately felt stupid. Of course he liked it, or he wouldn't spend so much time around airplanes.

But he took my question seriously. "I *love* to fly," he said. "If you decide to go up this afternoon, I think you'll see why." Josh ducked under the wing of the little plane and pulled open the door. "Why don't we all get in, and I'll show you a few things."

It was just like getting into Annie's Volkswagen. She got in first and slid into the back. "I sit up front all the time," she told me.

I slipped across the cockpit to the copilot's seat, while Josh climbed into the pilot's seat beside me.

"This is a dual-control plane," Josh explained, "just like the big ones you've ridden in." He pulled on the steering wheel, turning it from side to side.

"I see," I said, even though I didn't understand at all. What I really noticed was the inadvertent brush of his hand against my bare thigh as he demonstrated the various features of the plane.

"The pedals control the rudder and the brake," he said.

I nodded.

He pointed to dials and gadgets on the dashboard. "On the flight panel," he said, "we've got the altimeter, the compass, the turn-and-bank indicator, the air speed indicator, the rate-of-climb indicator, the artificial horizon, and the tachometer."

I looked at him. "Is there a quiz afterward?"

He grinned. "I just want you to know that everything you see here is on the big planes, too. It's standard flying equipment."

"You've convinced me," I said. "Let's go." But what had really convinced me was the fact that I wanted him to keep on sitting beside me in the small plane, so close that our shoulders touched.

"Great!" he exclaimed. Climbing out, he began a slow walk around the plane, checking things out. He looked into the engine, ran his hand down the wing and along the edge of the propeller, and moved the flaps at the back of the wings and the tail.

"Is he always this thorough, or is he just trying to impress us?" I asked Annie as I fastened my shoulder harness.

"Are you kidding?" she said. "Pilots are very serious about this part of the flight. His dad does exactly the same thing every time he goes up."

Josh unchained the wings and pulled the blocks of wood out from under the wheels. Then, getting back in the cockpit, he turned the key until the engine coughed and the propeller began to whirl. Then he picked up a microphone and clicked it on.

"This is Cessna 127 to base," he said into the mike.

"Roger, Josh." It was Jumbo's nasal twang. "What's up?"

"We are," Josh said. "We're going up for about

thirty minutes for a fly-over. Any traffic in the area?"

"Negative. Have a good flight."

"Thanks, Jumbo. See you later. Out." Josh hung up the mike and revved the engine.

"You don't have to check with the control tower?" I asked.

Josh laughed. "What control tower? The airport's too small for that. Jumbo handles the radio. That's pretty much all we need."

I held tightly to the seat as we rolled across the apron toward the runway and taxied to the end. Josh turned the plane around, and a second later the engine roared, and my stomach tightened. He released the brake, and we began to speed quickly down the runway. My stomach was rumbling with the racing, bumpy, movement, but halfway to the end of the runway, we stopped bouncing and began to rise smoothly. We were flying.

Josh turned the plane to the south. Behind us Annie said something, but I couldn't hear her over the noise of the engine. Josh leaned close to me. "That's Vermilion," he said, pointing to my right. Looking out under the wing, I could see the town, the tidy squares of its streets blurred by green trees. Further west, Lake Vermilion was a large silver saucer dotted with toy boats. Directly below, the fields were a green-and-yellow checkerboard, marked with red-roofed barns and neat white houses. Here and there herds of miniature cows were grazing. On the earth below, everything was ordered, arranged. But above and beyond was the open sky. As I turned my head to look around, the clear blue stretched endlessly in every direction, and I suddenly felt bouyant and free. I must have been smiling, because when I glanced over at Josh, I caught him watching me, grinning. Then he nodded, just a little, and turned his attention to the plane again.

In that moment I felt he had read my thoughts. I felt my cheeks reddening again, and I looked away quickly, out to the west, where the edge of the prairie melted into the edge of the sky. To be flying in such a small plane like this, with everything so open—I'd never felt anything like it. I guess I'd always been pretty practical. I had always had a good idea of what would happen next—senior year at Vermilion, then college, then law school. But up here . . . I felt anything could happen. It was thrilling and dangerous, and I loved it.

It's just a plane ride, I reminded myself. Nothing is different.

But I think I knew, down inside, that something *was* different. Something was happening, something I didn't want to acknowledge, even to myself.

4

I WAS SILENT MOST OF THE WAY BACK TO TOWN. MY heart had stopped pounding, but I still felt shivery and I knew my cheeks were flushed.

"And did you notice"—Annie skidded around the corner as she spoke—"how he handled the plane? He really knows his stuff."

"Would you mind slowing down a little?" I said, wishing she'd talk about something else. Hearing her talk about Josh was making me uncomfortable. "Your Volkswagen doesn't have wings, you know."

"Oops, sorry." Annie took her foot off the accelerator. "I wasn't paying attention. I just get so excited when I go flying with Josh. Wasn't it fun?"

"Uh-huh," I said absently.

She glanced at me. "Are you okay, Lauren? Your face is kind of flushed."

"I'm okay," I said. "I guess I'm still a little shaky, that's all. I'm not exactly used to flying every day."

Having a crush on my best friend's boyfriend wasn't something that happened every day of the

34

week, either. If that's what it was. But surely it wasn't. Surely I wouldn't go and do a dumb thing like that. Anyway, I was the one who didn't believe in love at first sight.

Annie nodded. "Hey, you haven't told me what you think of him." She sighed. "Isn't he wonderful? Isn't he the most perfect guy you ever met?"

"He's really cute," I agreed cautiously. "And he does seem to know a lot about planes."

Annie frowned. "You don't sound very enthusiastic about him."

"What do you want me to say? He's super? He's the most fabulous guy I've ever seen?"

"I know you'll get to like him," Annie said serenely. "Listen, why don't you go out with us Friday night? He's taking me to the hot air balloon race at the airport. There are fireworks afterward."

"I don't know," I said doubtfully. "I'd probably feel like a fifth wheel." Actually I was torn. The idea of seeing Josh again made me feel flushed and warm. I wanted to spend more time with him, but at the same time, I felt afraid. "Anyway," I added, "Josh probably wouldn't want me tagging along."

"Lauren Michaels, what's wrong with you?" Annie asked. "Josh likes you. I could tell by the way he talks to you. Of course he'll want you to go out with us."

I sighed. It would probably be easier to go out with them than to try to make excuses. Anyway, I was sure that my silly infatuation—because that's all it was, all it *could* be—would fade in a couple of days. Then I'd be back to normal, and we'd all have fun together.

"Okay," I agreed. "I'll go."

"Great," Annie said enthusiastically. "Hey, how about stopping for a hamburger before we go home? For some reason flying always makes me hungry."

The trouble was that my silly infatuation didn't fade, and I didn't get back to normal. On Friday evening Annie and Josh came to get me in Josh's pickup truck—an ancient green Dodge he called Max—and we went to the airport to watch the hot air balloons. A lot of townspeople were having picnics on the grass, including Dad, Carolyn, Maggie, Aunt Ruth, and Uncle Paul. We ate with them while we listened to the Vermilion High School band play pieces like "The Colonel Bogey March" and "Stars and Stripes Forever."

The balloons rose into the early evening sky like colored glass bubbles, floating in the twilight while we lay on the grass and watched. Annie and Josh talked idly, and I joined the conversation from time to time. But I couldn't really feel part of it. There was too much going on inside me.

It was torture to lie so close to Josh. When he turned his face to me to say something, I had to suppress the urge to touch the corner of his mouth, to move closer to him, to lie against his warm body on the grass.

I was also acutely aware that Annie was lying on the other side of him, pressed against him. It was dark now, and the fireworks were going off. When I propped myself up on my elbows, I could see her hand reaching for his, his fingers curling around hers. Then I saw her bend over Josh to kiss him. His hand came up, his fingers caught in her short hair, and he pulled her face to his. The sky filled with the brilliant shower of a Roman candle, illuminating their long kiss, and I moved away, feeling self-conscious and terribly alone.

Maybe that was it, I told myself—maybe that aloneness was what accounted for the way I felt about Josh. Maybe it was leaving Rich and my other friends; maybe it was the wedding. Everything in my life was new, and I hadn't had a say in any of it. I'd been plunked down in the middle of a new family I didn't want to be in, in a town a thousand miles from where I'd spent my whole life, and I was going to be starting a new school. . . . Maybe that was what was making me want to be closer to Josh. Somehow, the thought made me feel a little better. If that was the source of my feelings—well, it was only a matter of time before I'd get over them. But still, I was glad when the band played "The Star-Spangled Banner," and it was time to go home.

On the way to the parking lot I had a new dilemma. I could tell that Annie wanted some time with Josh alone, even though she hadn't said anything. I didn't blame her. If I were her, I would have felt the same way. So, when we climbed into Josh's truck, I was careful to sit on the outside.

"I'm pretty tired. Why don't you take me home first?" I suggested.

"I was thinking that we might go to Randy's and

get banana splits," Josh said. He look inquiringly at Annie.

"That sounds great," Annie said, slipping her arm across Josh's shoulders.

What could I do but agree? We went to Randy's, a popular hangout that was plastered with Vermilion High pennants and pictures of the basketball team that had won the state championship fourteen years before. While we ate our ice cream, we talked lightly about the evening. When we'd finished, Josh dropped me off at my house before going on to Annie's.

I was just about to open the door when he said, "Hey, Annie, maybe Lauren would like to go to the lake with us tomorrow." Without waiting for her to answer, he leaned over and said to me, "My brother's got this dinky little sailboat that's just big enough for two people. It's a lot of fun, especially when the wind comes up. How about it?"

I couldn't help smiling at him. It figured that a guy who liked flying planes would also like sailing the tiniest boat he could find—and in the windiest weather! It wouldn't be much fun for three. And I wasn't at all sure that I wanted to spend a whole afternoon watching Annie make out with Josh. Tonight had been bad enough. Worse yet, I had the feeling that Annie didn't want me to barge in on her date. She seemed a little slow in seconding Josh's invitation. But then she said, "Yes, Lauren, you have to." I didn't have a good reason not to— at least, not any reason I could give them—so I agreed, and we said good-night.

When I got inside the house, I passed Dad and

Carolyn at the kitchen table holding hands. I didn't stop to talk. I went upstairs, brushed my teeth, put on my pajamas, and climbed into bed. But I couldn't sleep. I lay in the dark, watching the shadows of the maple trees dancing on the wall and thinking about Josh and Annie and what they were probably doing at that very moment.

Finally I drifted off. I dreamed that I was watching Annie and Josh standing beside the plane, locked in each other's arms, kissing passionately. When I looked again, I saw that it wasn't Annie and Josh, but Dad and Carolyn, their arms wrapped around each other. Then Maggie was suddenly beside me. "My turn!" she cried. "My turn!"

I knew just how she felt. I woke up feeling more miserable than ever. My life was one big mess.

The next afternoon on the way to meet Josh at the lake, while Josh and his younger brother were out sailing, I got a detailed report from Annie of what had happened after they'd dropped me off the night before. She spared me none of the romantic details. I tried to be excited for her, but I was relieved when we finally got there and Annie and Josh went out in the boat, and I didn't have to hear any more. I had plenty of time to dig my toes into the hot sand and think. But all I could seem to think about was what Annie had said, the way she and Josh had been close together in his truck, losing themselves in each other's arms.

I couldn't fault her for feeling the way she did about Josh. She had every reason for falling in love with him and for wanting to tell me about it down to the last passionate detail. After all, what were best friends for? I couldn't exactly tell her to keep her romantic escapades to herself.

I sat up and dabbed more sunscreen on my nose. The worst of it was, that while she could tell me what she was feeling, I couldn't tell *her*. I couldn't say, "I'm wildly attracted to your boyfriend, and sometimes I wish you'd go away and leave him free for me."

Josh and Annie came back from sailing, and then it was my turn to go on the boat. I felt pretty uncomfortable about it, so I suggested that Annie go out again, but she said she wanted to lie on the sand. I couldn't think of any other excuses, so Josh and I waded into the water, shoved the little boat out to catch the wind, and climbed on.

Josh sailed the boat the way he flew his plane, with a competence that made even the trickiest maneuvers look simple. He guided the little boat so that it went flying as fast as it could, and it was obvious he loved the challenge. I was clinging anxiously to the side of the sailboat, but I was glad that the wind was blowing hard enough to keep him busy with the sail and the tiller. I couldn't think of a thing to say to him, and anyway, I was too breathless to speak.

If it had been hard the night before, lying beside him on the grass, it was much harder now. This time we were alone, without Annie. I was agonizingly aware of his lean, tanned, body, the firm sureness of his hands closing over the lines and the tiller, the quick way he'd flash me a bright smile from time to time. His bare feet touching mine sent a shiver through my body. The thoughts that came into my head were so surprising that they left me speechless and trembling.

I couldn't get rid of the tingling feeling, but after a little while I found my voice. We talked about boats—I'd sailed several summers on the Potomac—and about the sails and the wind and the way the boat responded. I relaxed and started enjoying myself. Josh said, "Hey, why don't you take it for a little while?" As he climbed across me so that I could slide back along the seat and take the tiller, he was so close that I could feel his warm breath and the brush of his soft skin against my shoulder. Luckily the wind came up much harder just then, kicking up the whitecaps and heeling us over, so that I had to concentrate on the boat. It was a challenge to hold it steady against the wind while we hiked out to the side to balance it, laughing and shouting, our water-slicked arms and bodies thrown together. It felt so natural and exhilarating. For those moments there seemed to be just the two of us, alone on the lake, alone with the boat and the wind. Alone and free.

But then I looked back at the beach and saw Annie waving, and the illusion faded. We weren't alone. Josh wasn't free. And neither was I. He was Annie's boyfriend, and I was her best friend.

In the next two weeks, I had even more occasions to remind myself that Josh belonged to Annie. As the days went on, I had to work hard to hide my feelings—from both of them.

One afternoon I'd finally had enough. By then

the three of us had spent another afternoon at the lake, taken a canoe trip to Kickapoo State Park, and spent an evening at a drive-in movie. Each time I'd been terribly conscious, in an intensely *physical* way, of Josh's presence, and I was feeling more and more ill at ease. So, when Annie asked me to go to the county livestock show with them, I said no.

"But I'm only trying to show you how easy it is to have fun in Vermilion." She said it jokingly, but I could tell she was a little hurt.

"I think," I said dryly, "that I've got the general idea."

"And I know things aren't exactly fun at your house just now," Annie added, "what with Maggie, I mean. It's good for you to get out a little."

"I've been getting out a *lot*," I said. "Even in Washington I didn't get out this much. It's time I took a rest."

The simplest thing, of course, would have been to tell her what the problem was. But it was too embarrassing. Anyway, what could I have said? "Listen, Annie, you'll never believe this, but I've got the world's most gigantic crush on your boyfriend."

No. I couldn't say it. The whole thing was utterly, absolutely, hopeless. The less said about it the better.

So, I said again, "Thanks for the invitation, but I'm going to beg off."

"Josh will be disappointed," Annie said, firing her last shot.

I sighed. That wasn't what I wanted to hear—and yet it was. Everything was so mixed up.

"Thanks anyway," I said firmly. "But no thanks."

On the home front things were almost as complicated. Carolyn and Dad were still at the honeymoon-romance stage, which annoyed Maggie no end. "Gooey gush," she would announce loudly, making a terrible face whenever she caught them kissing or holding hands.

At first Dad tried to laugh it off. "You've got quite a way with words, Maggie," he'd say, and reach out his hand to ruffle her hair affectionately. Maggie would jerk away from him.

She did something else that would have been funny if it hadn't been so sad. She was always trying to put herself between Dad and Carolyn. Sometimes it was almost comic, watching her make a mad dash to the car so she could sit in the middle of the front seat, or seeing her wriggle between them when they sat together on the sofa in front of the television. Carolyn would try to get her to sit somewhere else, but Maggie would cram herself between them, glowering. Although I didn't approve of how unbearably obnoxious she was being, I understood it. If I'd been ten years old, I might have been doing the same thing.

It was just as difficult for me to adjust to Carolyn. I'd been twelve when Mom died, and in the five years since, I'd pretty much handled things at home, doing the laundry, cleaning, and cooking. Now, of course, it was different. Carolyn had taken over. I had known this would happen for almost a year, but I still felt unprepared. I didn't miss the chores, of course, but I missed the sense of responsibility. I guess it made me feel important.

Worse yet, Carolyn was making it pretty clear that she wanted to be my mother. "But I already had a mother," I wanted to scream at her. I was only going to be here one more year, and then I'd be away at college, and we could all forget this stuff about being a family. A family was a father and mother and kids—and Carolyn just wasn't my mother, no matter how much she might want to be. I avoided her offers to go shopping and do things together whenever I could, but a big blowup finally brought the problems bubbling to the surface where we could all see them.

One evening I came home from Annie's house to find Maggie in my room, stealthily going through my drawers. She'd already found my most precious treasure—my mother's square-cut emerald pendant—and she was wearing it around her neck.

"Take that off!" I yelled, furious. "Nobody wears that but me!"

"I didn't hurt it," Maggie said sullenly, fumbling with the catch.

"I don't care," I said. "Take it off!" Of all my mother's jewelry, it was by far my favorite. Whenever I looked at it, I thought of the way she had looked wearing it, regal and beautiful. I had vowed that nobody but me would ever put it on.

When the pendant was safe in my drawer, I grabbed Maggie by the arm, dragged her to the kitchen, and plunked her down on a chair in front of Carolyn and my dad.

"Would you please tell this *child*," I said icily, "to stay out of my room? I caught her going through my drawers."

"Maggie!" Carolyn exclaimed. "How could you do a thing like that?"

"It was easy," Maggie said, tossing her head. "I just opened the door and walked in and turned on the light—"

"That's enough, young lady," Dad told her. "Don't be flippant with your mother."

Maggie turned on him. "I don't have to take orders from you, Sam!"

"Yes, you do!" Carolyn said. "And you're not to call him Sam, either."

Maggie folded her arms, and thrust her chin forward. "You can't make me call him Dad," she said defiantly. "He's not my father!"

Dad tried making a joke out of it. "The man who applies for *that* job," he remarked mildly, "would certainly have his hands full."

Maggie stomped her foot. Tears were beginning to stream down her face, and her mouth was twisted. "I hate living in this family!" she cried. "It's *defunct*!"

Carolyn and Dad exchanged raised-eyebrow glances. They were obviously trying not to smile. "I think you mean *dysfunctional*, honey," Carolyn suggested.

"That's right," Maggie said in a haughty tone. "I heard about it on television. We've got a dys— dysfunctional family."

"And what exactly is that?" I asked coldly. "A

family where people go through other people's drawers?"

Maggie pulled herself up to her full height, all four feet nine inches of it. Her blond braids stuck out on either side of her head. "A dysfunctional family," she said, "is one where the people hate one another."

"But we don't hate one another," Carolyn said.

"Yes, we do!" Maggie shouted furiously. "Lauren hates you and me, Sam hates me, and I hate Sam and Lauren!" With that she stormed out of the room, slamming the door so hard that an antique sugar bowl fell off one of the cupboard shelves and shattered on the floor.

There was an awkward pause. "Well," my father said after a moment, "Maggie seems to have covered most of the bases." He glanced at Carolyn. "Did she leave anybody out?"

Carolyn shook her head. She was picking up the pieces of the sugar bowl, turning them over in her fingers. "Maybe I can mend it," she said.

"Maggie seems to have gotten off scot-free," I pointed out in an acid tone. "Isn't anybody going to punish her for going through my drawers?"

Dad pulled me against him in a hug, the way he used to when I was a little girl. "You have to be patient, honey. Maggie's having a difficult time adjusting to being part of a family." He looked down at me thoughtfully. "You know, it might help if you didn't take her so seriously, if you tried to develop a sense of humor." Turning to Carolyn, he asked, "Do you think we're a defunct family?"

Carolyn sighed. "I'll confess to worrying about it from time to time."

I pulled away from my father, still feeling miffed. "You're not going to do anything to keep her out of my room?"

Carolyn gave me an apologetic smile. "I'll talk to her, Lauren," she promised. "She won't do it again."

"And you might try working on that sense of humor," Dad added. "If we're fated to be defunct, we might as well go down laughing." He reached for Carolyn's hand, and they both giggled like a couple of kids.

The gesture only made me angrier. As I left the kitchen, I said crossly, "I guess I'll go upstairs and work on my sense of humor."

5

MERCIFULLY, SCHOOL STARTED RIGHT AFTER THAT, and we could all get away from one another. But I was afraid that it was going to be like that old saying: out of the frying pan and into the fire. I had to face a new school, get used to new teachers, make new friends—settle into a whole new way of life. If I'd stayed in Washington, I could have coasted through my senior year. But here I had to start all over again. To tell the truth, I was scared.

Vermilion High was as different from Franklin High as it could be. Instead of two thousand students, there were only three hundred. Everything was a lot smaller. There were only a couple of square buildings with wings and annexes set on a few acres of green lawn, where there was a football field and a few playing fields. The dusty parking lot was crammed with yellow school buses, battered old pickup trucks, and motorbikes.

Almost without exception, everybody wore jeans. The guys wore T-shirts, and the girls wore blouses or sweaters. Only a handful of girls were dressed up, even on the first day.

That morning I had decided I should wear an outfit that would be a hit. I wanted to make an impression on my first day of school. I dug around in my closet and found an outfit that all my friends had admired the year before, a long paisley skirt and an olive-green top, with olive leather lace-up boots. I looped my hair off to one side and fastened it with a gold comb, so that it fell down around my shoulders in a cascade of dark curls. When I looked at myself in the mirror, I knew I looked great. A touch of green eye shadow was the only thing needed to make it just right.

But I was wrong. Just about all the girls had on jeans and casual tops. It was pretty obvious I was the only new student in the senior class, which wasn't very big to begin with. Back at Franklin High, outside my small circle of close friends, I'd felt almost totally anonymous. But here I felt as if there were neon arrows pointing at me everywhere I went, and I wasn't sure I liked it. Everybody was curious about me—some in a friendly way, others who just stood around and gawked, as if I were a creature from another planet. I had the feeling that it was going to take me months to fit in, if ever. And the big question in my mind was, did I want to? It was sort of like the feeling I had about living with Maggie and Carolyn. I'd only be here one more year, and then I'd go away to college. Maybe it wasn't worth trying to fit in. But still, things weren't hopeless. A couple of cute guys smiled at me, and I had the feeling that my outfit, outlandish as some of the girls seemed to think it was, had caught a few looks from the boys.

Luckily, Annie's locker was next to mine, right in the middle of the main hall—front row center, so to speak. On that first morning she kept dragging kids over to introduce them to me. It made me a little uncomfortable, since most of them were guys. Annie's ulterior motive—to make sure that I had a date for the next Friday night—was pretty obvious. Anyway, in ten minutes, I'd probably met a third of the senior class.

By the time David Maloney came along, I was glad to see a familiar face. He looked really cute, with his sun-bleached hair and dark tan. I liked the way his brown eyes lit up when he saw me. I'd spent the past few weeks feeling on the outside of several closed circles. David was somebody who would include me in.

"How were the Rockies?" I asked him.

"They were great. How about your summer? How do you like living in Vermilion?"

"She'll like it more with you here," Annie put in helpfully.

I stiffened, feeling embarrassed by the blatant hint.

David, however, didn't seem to mind.

"What lunch period do you have?" he asked me in his steady midwestern drawl.

I consulted my new schedule. "Fourth."

"Me, too. How about having lunch together? You can tell me everything that happened while I was gone."

"Sure," I said.

He grinned at me. "Hey, by the way, I like your outfit." After David had sauntered off, Annie turned to me with a wide smile. "I can see that things are getting off to a good start."

"No big deal," I said, putting my new gym clothes into my locker. "Want to eat with us?"

Annie shook her head. "You don't understand, Lauren. Around here, when a guy asks a girl to have lunch with him, or even to walk with him to class, it *is* a big deal. It's almost like a date. Anyway, I've got math fourth period, so I guess we won't be having lunch together."

I raised my eyebrows. Walking to class was a date? Strange places, strange customs. But at that moment, Josh walked up, flashing one of his big, wide, smiles, and all thoughts of David and lunch and strange customs flew out of my mind.

"Hi, Annie. Hi, Lauren," he said. He looked at me, and his glance seemed to linger on my mouth, to draw me closer. I was conscious of the muscles under his blue shirt, of the easy, relaxed, way he walked. I thought for a moment of how our bodies had been thrown together in the boat, and I felt my face grow hot.

I turned back to my locker, hoping Annie hadn't noticed my flaming cheeks. Josh gave Annie a quick hug and then looked back at me.

"Have you figured out where your homeroom is, Lauren?"

I looked at my schedule. "I've got Ms. Ryan," I said. "Room 208."

"I've got Mr. Daily, out at the end of the west wing," Annie told him. "And after that, computer literacy, still in the west wing. Who've you got for homeroom?"

"Ryan." He smiled at me, and my heart leaped. "We're in the east wing, second floor, Lauren. Want me to show you?"

I nodded wordlessly. Was he asking me on kind of a date? Of course not, since he was my best friend's boyfriend. It had just been a friendly gesture, common sense told me. But my heart kept hoping it was something else.

"Good. See you at lunch." Annie grabbed her computer book and headed off in one direction, while Josh and I turned in the other.

Friendly gesture or not, I was ridiculously happy. It was an incredible high just being with Josh, walking beside him, alone with him for the first time since we'd sailed together over two weeks ago. His arm casually brushed against mine as we went up the stairs, making me feel completely giddy. And when we got to room 208 and he held open the door and smiled down at me, my heartbeat went crazy.

My imagination was running wild. I could imagine him kissing my mouth, my throat. I could imagine the two of us in the boat again, under the blazing heat of the sun, bare-limbed, our bodies close together. I could imagine—

But I had to *stop* imagining. My imagination was turning my knees to water and making my breath come in little gasps. If I didn't stop, I'd fall into his arms and make an utter fool of myself. This was crazy! I'd never felt this way about a guy before, but every time I was with Josh, it was the same way. It wasn't at all like me to feel so shivery and out of control. I was actually glad when I could sit down and try to get hold of myself.

As it turned out, Josh and I had English together the following period, and he walked me to that class, too. By then I'd had time to get my act together. I was able to talk rationally and keep a rein on my silly imagination. I asked all about Vermilion High, and about him.

"There's not much to tell, really," Josh told me. "I guess you figured out by now that I'm into sports, especially flying. I'm sports editor on the *Star*, too. That's the school paper." He laughed a little self-consciously and added, "It probably doesn't seem like much compared to what you're used to."

"That's not true," I told him, and I meant it. He talked so enthusiastically, it was obvious that he put a lot of thought and energy into the things he did, that they meant a lot to him.

"I used to be on the basketball team, too," he went on. "But I hurt my ankle last year, and had to give it up. Anyway," he said with a laugh, "there wasn't enough room for both flying *and* basketball in my life."

We were outside the English classroom now, but we were still a few minutes early, so we stood outside and kept talking. Josh leaned one arm against the wall and bent toward me, asking, "Have you thought about getting involved with any activities here?"

I shook my head, thinking how incredibly handsome he looked. "Not yet." I told him how, back at Franklin, I'd been on the debating team. I was sure he'd think it was boring and dry, but he asked me all kinds of questions about it.

"Vermilion doesn't have a debating team," he explained. "But maybe you should think about joining the paper. It would be fun to have you on it, too."

I felt a thrill when he suggested that. We talked a little more, and I found myself thinking of all the new and different kinds of things I could get involved in at Vermilion, instead of all the things I'd left behind at Franklin High. I also found myself thinking that Josh Reynolds was much more than just an incredibly gorgeous guy. He was caring and smart and thoughtful, too. We lingered outside the English classroom for so long that we were almost late.

But once English class began, I had time to think about what had just happened. The more I thought, the guiltier I felt about talking to Josh. No, it was more complicated than that. I was feeling guilty about feeling the way I felt when I talked to Josh—breathless and giddy with happiness—and I was feeling disloyal to Annie, too. Accepting a friendly gesture, imagining a few romantic scenes—that was one thing. But when we were talking, I'd gotten the feeling that things might go beyond "just friendly," and that couldn't happen. From now on, I told myself sternly, I'd walk to class with somebody else.

The rest of the morning was pretty uneventful. A few kids introduced themselves and helped me find my way to the gym. Some wanted to know what it was like going to high school in Washington. The teachers were very nice, too; they knew everybody's name, and they seemed genuinely helpful. Some of the older ones had probably taught the kids' mothers and fathers. I discovered pretty quickly that even though my studies clearly weren't going to be a breeze, I wasn't lost, either. I'd have plenty of homework to do, but there'd be time for other things. The debating team was out, since there wasn't one, and so was the paper, I told myself firmly, since Josh was on it. But I was sure I'd find something fun to do.

At noon David was waiting for me inside the cafeteria. We got our lunches and sat down at a table. He told me all about his trip to the Rockies and asked about Washington and what I used to do there. I found myself enjoying his company. Perhaps if I let myself get involved with him, I would forget about Josh. And anyway, Annie would be pleased if I went out with David. So I said yes immediately when he suggested that we go to the football game together on Friday night.

I noticed, when he walked me to economics, that kids kept stopping to say hi to David. So he wasn't only cute and friendly, he was popular, too! As I settled down to hear Mr. Higgins' view of money and how it should be spent, I felt I was on the right track again.

Annie was glad too when I told her about my date with David, and was immediately full of plans. I could sleep over at her house, she said, and we could double-date to the game. Afterward we could all go back to her house and have something to eat. She was sure Josh would be glad to agree because he liked David. I started to say that I wasn't sure I wanted to double-date, but, as usual, when Annie was set on something, it was impossible to change her mind, so I gave in. Anyway, with David there, I was positive that I would have myself under control. I wouldn't feel three was a crowd, the way I'd felt before.

David stopped by my locker every morning that week to talk to me before class. We ate lunch together every day, and then he walked me to economics. On Thursday he held my hand as we walked. On Friday he slipped his arm around me and gave me a quick kiss before I went into the classroom. Our spending time together didn't escape the attention of the other kids, and by the end of the first week of school, we were being treated as a couple. Neither David nor I did anything to contradict that. David wasn't Josh, but Josh wasn't available. I even found myself looking forward to our date on Friday night. There was only one problem. Josh still walked me to homeroom every morning.

Sometimes he casually draped an arm around my shoulders or took my hand and swung it as we walked. Nobody seemed to give his actions a second thought.

Nobody except me, that is. I could still feel his arm on my shoulders while Mr. Hayes carried on about English romantic poetry. My fingers kept tingling long after he had dropped my hand after an encouraging squeeze before my first quiz. My heart kept pounding, my breath was still short, and my imagination was running wild. I could feel Josh's mouth warm and sweet on mine, even though his lips had only accidentally brushed my cheek when he whispered to me just before homeroom one day. I could feel the intensity of his look, the promise of it, even though he'd only tossed me a laughing glance as he turned away.

Through it all I kept reminding myself that Josh was Annie's boyfriend. He was only being kind to me because I was her cousin and because I was new in town. It was my imagination that was conjuring up all this other stuff.

The odd thing was that as the week went on, the real world and the world of my imagination seemed to get confused. Surely I was imagining it—and yet Josh's eyes *did* linger on mine when we said good-bye and parted for our classes. He *did* stand very close to me, so close that I could feel the warmth of his body. And Friday morning he'd started to say something to me in a voice that held a note of deep seriousness and then stopped himself, almost as if he'd been afraid to go on.

What had he been about to say? Was it possible that these touches, this closeness *weren't* my imagination? Had Josh begun to feel some of the things I was feeling? When that idea came to me, I felt suddenly excited and hopeful.

But I was headed into dangerous territory, and I didn't want to go there. I had to stop myself. Josh was Annie's boyfriend, and I was her best friend. No amount of imagining, no amount of pretending, was going to change that.

On Friday I went over to Annie's house to get

ready for the game. The evening was cool for a change, and I'd talked Annie into dressing up. We changed into skirts and sweaters and low heels. I brushed my dark hair down around my shoulders, then tied it back with a narrow red velvet ribbon. I was dressing to look nice for David, I told myself. But as I took a final check of my makeup in the mirror, I knew in my heart that was a lie.

David and Josh arrived at about the same time, David driving an old yellow Buick, Josh, as usual, in his green truck.

When David saw me, he gave a wide, appreciative smile. "Hey, nice." He slipped his arm around my shoulders.

"Yeah," Josh agreed. He gave Annie a kiss, but I could have sworn that his gaze lingered on me, that his wide grin was meant for me, too.

Grabbing my bag, I went determinedly over to David and said, "Well, I guess we should go." But it wasn't until David and I were in his Buick, apart from Josh and Annie in Josh's truck, that I calmed down and could trust myself to act normally.

The evening began better than I'd hoped. I'd never really enjoyed football. Most of the kids at Franklin High didn't really get involved in it because there was so much else to do. But here in Vermilion the games were a big deal, a community affair, really. The bleachers around the football field—you couldn't call it a stadium—were crammed with teenagers and parents and lots of little kids shoulder-to-shoulder.

When the band marched onto the field for its pregame show, everybody yelled excitedly. But when the cheerleaders cartwheeled onto the field and the Vermilion Hustlers followed in their maroon-and-white uniforms, that's when the fans really went crazy. The bleachers erupted with cheering and foot stamping, and maroon-and-white pom-poms blossomed all over the place. It was the loudest, most excited, crowd I'd ever seen. Every touchdown against the visiting Bismarck Blue Devils sparked an incredible celebration, each louder and rowdier than the last. When the game was over, the Hustlers had beaten the Blue Devils, 21–14, and we were all hoarse from cheering at the top of our lungs and bone weary from jumping up and down. I'd honestly had a good time.

Afterward the four of us drove back to Annie's house, where Aunt Ruth had left us the makings for a late supper—sandwiches and chips and plenty of soft drinks. We put an old movie on the VCR in the den and ate in front of the TV, laughing and joking. I felt relaxed and happy.

After we'd eaten, Annie turned out all the lights but the one in the hallway, and we settled down to watch the film. Annie and Josh were sitting on the sofa, while David and I had the loveseat.

In the semidarkness I could tell that Josh and Annie were getting pretty passionate. Before, the kisses I had seen must have been censored, and I'd only had Annie's reports of what went on when I wasn't there. Now I could see out of the corner of my eye that their kisses were more than playful or teasing. Locked in each other's arms, they appeared to be utterly oblivious of David and me.

With a chuckle David pulled me closer to him.

"I don't think we need to worry about having an audience," he said in a low voice. "It looks like they're occupied."

I nodded, forcing myself to look away. David leaned forward and kissed me, sweetly and gently. It was the kiss I'd been anticipating for the past few days. It was a kiss that said, *I like you very much, Lauren; I could maybe even love you if you'd let me.* It was a nice kiss, but it wasn't the kiss that would help me put Josh out of my mind and my heart. I pressed myself against David, making the kiss deeper, harder. I felt him draw in his breath, as if he were surprised, and then he tightened his arms around me. I could feel his heart beating against my chest, hear his breath quicken, ragged in his throat. I let him pull me even closer, let his hand slide up my body, willing myself to forget Josh, to lose myself in David's kiss.

And I did, but only for a moment. Then I heard Josh groan, and Annie murmured, "Oh, Josh, I love you so much."

Suddenly all my feelings, all my imaginings about Josh ran headlong into reality. A searing flash of white-hot jealousy sliced through me like a lightning bolt. I couldn't sit there and listen to Josh kissing Annie—it hurt too much. I braced myself against the sharp pain.

Of course, David didn't have any idea what was going on inside my head. He felt me pull away and stiffen, and I knew he thought that our kiss had gone too far. He put his finger under my chin and said softly, "Hey, Lauren, I'm sorry. I guess I just got carried away." He pulled in his breath, laughing a little. "You've got quite an effect on a guy, you know?"

I managed a smile and leaned back in David's arms, trying to relax. Then, in the half-light, I saw that Josh was watching us, and I felt my body grow taut again. It was bad enough that I could hear him and Annie, but the idea that Josh could hear David kiss me was too much—especially when I was using David's kisses to help me forget about Josh. I pulled away.

David frowned. "Are you okay, Lauren?" he asked in a low voice. "Listen, I didn't mean to make you upset. Can we just . . . ?"

"No, it's not that," I said. "I've . . . I've got a headache."

David looked genuinely concerned. "That's too bad," he said. "Listen, I've got some aspirin out in the car."

I shook my head. "No," I said, "when it gets this bad, the best thing I can do is go to bed." I bit my lip, feeling guilty that I'd lied. "I hope you don't mind, David."

"No, of course I don't mind. But I think you ought to do something for that headache."

There was a rustle on the sofa. "Headache?" Annie asked in a blurry voice. "Lauren, have you got a headache?"

"Yes." I was beginning to feel embarrassed. I hadn't meant to cause such a ruckus, but there wasn't anything I could do about it now. And I definitely didn't want to stay in the same room with Josh and Annie.

I stood up. "I'm sorry to break this up, but I think I'd better go upstairs to bed."

David got to his feet. "I guess I'll be going, too," he said. "Listen, you guys, I've had a great time. Thanks for the food, Annie."

Josh cleared his throat. "I hope your headache's nothing serious, Lauren."

"I'll be okay," I replied. "I just need some sleep." By this time I was feeling like an utter idiot. Why hadn't I just ignored Josh and let David kiss me? Why hadn't I suggested that he and I go sit in the car and talk, where we could be by ourselves? Why had I made such a big deal about Josh's watching? Maybe he hadn't actually been watching anyway. Maybe I'd overreacted. But I couldn't undo what I had done. I couldn't pretend that my headache had magically disappeared, either. David kissed me good-night quickly. After he left, I went upstairs.

Five minutes later I heard Josh driving away, too, and Annie came upstairs with a bottle of aspirin in one hand and a glass of water in the other.

"Do you really feel bad?" she asked. I felt a pang of guilt at her concern. If she only knew the real reason I felt awful. "Here. Take these."

"I'm okay," I said. "Sorry I broke up the evening."

Annie sat down on the bed. "Is everything all right? Did David do something you didn't want him to? Is there anything you want to talk about?"

Now was my chance. I could lie to her—it would be easy to tell her that David's kiss had been too passionate for a first date. Or I could tell her the truth, the *real* truth. I hesitated, wanting to confess to her and get rid of the awful burden I was carrying. But I couldn't bring myself to say the words. Finally I just shook my head. She was so sweet. It would destroy all her trust in me if I told her how I felt about Josh. I knew I was wrong to care for him. I was wrong to feel jealous. I was wrong to be disloyal to Annie. And the knowledge of how wrong I was made me feel awful. But I couldn't think of anything to say, or any way to make myself stop loving him.

Annie smoothed the hair from my forehead. "Well, if you need anything," she said getting up, "just let me know." Then she went into the bathroom to brush her teeth.

I lay in the bed, stiff and taut. By then I really did have a headache.

6

I HAD TO GO HOME ON SATURDAY MORNING, SO ANNIE and I didn't have a lot of time to talk about the night before. For once, I was glad Carolyn had an outing planned for us, even though it meant spending an utterly boring day in Springfield with her. At least I didn't have to worry about running into Josh. And I was determined to keep it that way. Stay away from trouble, and it will stay away from you, as Aunt Ruth always said.

Instead of hanging around my locker Monday morning, I invented an errand that got me to school just before the bell so I could avoid walking to homeroom with Josh. After homeroom I found a sudden interest in talking to other kids, and I took a different route to English class. My efforts were so successful that I didn't talk to Josh all day. Strangely enough, I had the feeling that he might be going out of his way to keep from seeing me, too.

It was better this way. I had to keep telling myself that when I was tempted to linger at my locker and wait for Josh to show up.

When I saw David on Monday, I felt terrible about how I'd acted on Friday night and swore to myself that I'd make more of an effort to get to know him. We had lunch together as usual, and he was more charming and sweeter than ever. The seniors were planning a roller-skating party on Friday night, and he asked me to go with him.

"A skating party?" I asked doubtfully. "I don't know, David. I've never been on roller skates before. I've ice-skated a little, that's all."

David laughed. "I'm not very good, either, but it'll be a lot of fun. You'll see." He paused. "Maybe we could double with Josh and Annie. I'm sure they'll be going, too."

"Thanks," I said, "but why don't we go by ourselves? Would you mind?"

His brown eyes lit up. "Mind? I'd love to have you all to myself."

Annie cornered me that afternoon. "You don't want to double to the skating party?"

I managed a laugh. "News travels fast," I said. "How'd you hear that?"

"I ran into David and suggested that we go together. But he said you guys were going by yourselves. There's nothing wrong, is there?"

"Of course not," I said quickly. "It's just that . . . well, David and I are just getting to know each other. I thought it might be good if we had a little time to ourselves, that's all."

"I can understand." She smiled, apparently satisfied. "When Josh and I started dating, I guess I wouldn't have wanted to double. I would have hated to share him with anyone." She grinned. "Even my best friend."

I'd never been to a roller-skating rink before. It was a dizzying experience—all those kids, going around and around to the music, under a kaleido-scope of colored lights. Some needed all the help they could get to stay on their feet, so they were clinging to the rail, while others whipped in and out of the crowd, seeing how fast they could skate without getting a warning whistle from the moni-tor. The best ones were out in the middle of the rink showing off their fast turns and daring acro-batics. I wasn't in a class with them, of course, but I was pleased that I didn't have to hang on to the rail, either.

"Hey, you're not bad," David remarked, turning in front of me so that he was skating backward in time to the fast rhythm of the music.

"I thought you said you weren't very good," I said accusingly, watching his easy balance.

"I'm not," David replied. "At least not in com-parison to some of the others." He pointed. "Look."

I looked. Josh and Annie skated gracefully past us in synchronization, arms around each other, like dancers. I watched with envy as they made a cou-ple of swift, smooth turns. Annie was laughing up at Josh. But my breath caught in my throat when I saw that Josh was looking at David and me. There was something about the look. . . . It was so intense and searching.

"They're good, aren't they?" David asked.

"Yes," I said. I was afraid my voice would shake if I said anything more. I couldn't keep my eyes from following Josh's path around the rink. I hadn't talked to him all week. I hadn't even seen him except in class. I'd thought I'd finally managed to get my feelings under control. But I must have been wrong.

Josh whirled Annie around so that her back was toward us, and he was skating backward. He was still watching us—no, watching me, his eyes fastened on mine. I couldn't have been wrong. The look on his face was a look of longing. I recognized it because it exactly matched the way I felt. I was suddenly dizzy with the realization that Josh wanted me. It was true—it *had* to be true. My imagination couldn't have invented that look!

At that moment a big guy came up behind me, skating very fast. He started to veer around me, but he must have miscalculated, because he careened into me, sending me flying into the railing with a terrible crash. I saw stars, and the next thing I knew, I was sitting on the floor, my back propped against the railing, my feet sticking out in front of me. The guy was trying to apologize, and David was holding my hand. Suddenly Josh was kneeling beside me, too. His arm slid firmly around my shoulder, and I nearly fainted all over again, I was so shocked by how wonderful it felt.

"Lauren," he was saying urgently, "Lauren, are you all right?" There was a deep, anxious concern in his voice.

"Lauren?" It was Annie. "Lauren, are you okay? Nothing's broken?"

"I . . . I don't think so," I gasped. It hurt to breathe but only a little. "I guess I just got the breath knocked out of me."

"I'm really sorry," the guy who'd knocked me over muttered. "Guess I shouldn't have been going so fast."

"You're damn right, you idiot," Josh exclaimed angrily. "You could have *killed* her." He looked at me, and his voice softened. "You're sure you're all right?"

All right? I was more than all right. The look in Josh's eyes, the sound of his voice—I *hadn't* been imagining things! He *did* care for me! My heart was thudding in my chest.

"Can you get up?" Annie asked worriedly.

I nodded. But I wasn't looking at her. I was looking at Josh, and his eyes were telling me everything I needed to know.

I did a double take when David put his arm around my shoulders and helped pull me up; I'd almost forgotten that he was there. "Maybe we'd better sit the next one out," he said.

I shook my head. My ribs ached, but I'd never felt better in my life. "I think I'll just skate the kinks out," I said.

Josh grinned. "That-a-girl," he said. He hesitated, as if he wanted to say something else, but Annie was tugging at his arm.

"If Lauren's okay, we need to get moving," she said. "We're holding up traffic."

The small knot of people broke up, and David and I skated slowly around the floor. I saw that just about everybody was pairing off, boy-girl. The lights dimmed and the exhibition skaters left the middle of the rink. The music slowed and became soft and romantic.

"What's going on?" I asked.

"It's a change-couple skate. When the whistle blows, each guy skates to a different girl," David explained, "and so on, until all the guys have skated with all the girls." He made a face. "It's not exactly my favorite skate," he added. "It means that every guy gets to skate with my girlfriend."

I thought of asking him what he meant by "my girlfriend," but I was distracted by the thought that in a minute or two I'd be skating with Josh. My heart was still pounding, and I felt dazed. I cast a quick glance backward. Josh and Annie were behind us, three or four couples away.

David and I began to skate. After a time or two around the rink, there was a blast from the whistle. David squeezed my hand, waved, and skated on. Howie Hanson, a guy in my French class, took his place. After that it was a guy that everybody called Biff, and then tall, red-haired, Mitch Wilder, who asked me if I'd go to the movies with him the next week. I said no as nicely as I could.

"David's got you all sewed up, huh?" he asked, sounding disappointed.

"Um, well," I replied, hardly listening. I was still thinking about Josh and what had just happened. Mitch must have thought I said yes, because he shrugged and said, "Let me know if things change." Then the whistle blew, and he skated on.

The next thing I knew, a hand grasped mine and a firm arm slid around my waist. Those incredible blue eyes smiled down into mine, and white teeth flashed into a quick grin. My heart thudded.

"Hi, there," Josh said, matching his rhythm to mine.

There was an electric current flowing through our hands. I was immediately and intensely conscious that we were skating in perfect harmony, our strides matching, our bodies swaying to the beat of the music. I was conscious of his arm tight around my waist, of his hand holding mine. I didn't think about Annie. I'd forgotten all about David. I forgot everything except Josh. We didn't say anything. We didn't have to. Our bodies moving together said it all. The knowledge that Josh cared for me had changed everything.

As we skated, I let myself relax into Josh's arms, into the rhythm of the music. I smiled at him and he smiled back, as if he knew what I was thinking.

The whistle blew. I thought Josh was going to skate on, but he didn't.

"Let the next guy skate around," he said, his arm tightening around my waist. We skated another turn together without saying a word. Then the whistle blew again, Josh squeezed my hand, whispered, "Thanks," and was gone.

After that my mind was a blur. I was hardly aware of the other guys I skated with. Eventually David skated up again. I was still floating on a cloud as we went to get some soft drinks.

"Feeling okay after your spill?" David smiled at me. "You must be," he added, answering his own question. "You look pretty with your eyes shining that way."

I smiled back at him, feeling warm inside. "I'm more than okay," I said. "I'm having a wonderful time."

He bent over and kissed me, and I was feeling so joyful, so free from worry, that I kissed him back. I knew things weren't going to be easy. There was still plenty to deal with. I had to cope with the idea that the boy I loved belonged to my best friend. But just then I wasn't thinking of that. I was only thinking of how much I loved Josh. And at that moment everything seemed very simple.

By noon the next day, however, everything was complicated again.

I had just stepped out of the post office, where I'd mailed a package for Dad. It was beginning to drizzle and I pulled my sweater around me, wishing I'd had the good sense to bring a poncho. I was also thinking about Josh and wondering what he was doing. Then I saw, with a start, that his truck was parked in front of the post office, and that he was sitting behind the wheel. It was as if he had materialized out of my very thoughts.

Josh reached over and opened the passenger door for me. "I stopped at your house, looking for you," he called over to me. "Your mom said I'd find you here," he said.

I stared at him. He'd been looking for me? Had he come because he wanted to, or had Annie asked him to pick me up?

"Your hair's getting wet," he remarked. "Aren't you going to get in?"

I climbed into the passenger seat, feeling oddly

self-conscious. "Are we going over to Annie's?" I asked, closing the door.

"No," he said firmly. He turned the ignition key and put his truck into reverse, looking over his shoulder while he backed out of the parking space. "We're going someplace where we can talk."

I swallowed, remembering the night before, and the incredible happiness I'd felt with his arm around me. I was sure that he cared for me. But I knew he cared for Annie, too, and I knew that he was an honest, loyal, person. Had he come to tell me that we had to forget what had happened and put it behind us?

"Talk about what?" I finally choked out.

"About us." His mouth was set in a stern line and he didn't look at me. It began to rain harder and he flicked on the windshield wipers.

I swallowed again. He looked so serious. Now I *knew* what he was going to say, and there wasn't anything I could do to stop him. Worse, I knew that he was probably right. How had I thought it would be simple to love him? It was the most complicated thing in the world, and he would be right to tell me that we had to forget anything we felt for each other.

The Burger-Shake Drive-In was just around the corner, and Josh pulled in and rolled down his window. Pushing the button on the call box, he ordered two chocolate milk shakes. Then he rolled the window back up and faced me. I felt dizzy, almost faint.

"I've got a confession to make," he said very quietly. "I've been thinking about it for a few weeks now and trying to deal with it myself. But I can't handle it alone any longer. I've got to talk to you about it."

I could hear my breathing getting fast and shallow, and I gulped for air.

Josh leaned toward me, one tanned arm on the steering wheel. His blue eyes were on me, intent. "I'm in love with you, Lauren," he said.

For a few seconds I didn't think I'd heard right. I'd been so sure he was going to say something different. I closed my eyes and took a deep breath.

"I hope you're not angry with me for being blunt like this," he said. "But after last night at the rink— well, I guess I gave myself away. I stayed up all night trying to figure out what to do about it."

"I'm not angry," I said faintly.

He nodded. "It didn't just begin last night, but I guess I wasn't ready to be honest about it. In the beginning, those first couple of weeks, I tried telling myself that it wasn't happening, or that it was a silly kid's crush and it would go away. I thought it would fade. But it hasn't."

He paused and looked down. Our fingers were nearly touching on the seat of the truck. I wanted to reach for his hand, but I couldn't. I wanted to speak, but I felt frozen. I couldn't believe what I was hearing. It had to be a dream. In a minute I would wake up and he would be gone.

Then he put his hand over mine. It wasn't a dream.

"Then school started," he went on, "and things changed. I knew by then that it wasn't just a crush, and it wasn't going to go away. It was beginning to bother me. I mean, Annie's your cousin. I didn't want to cause trouble between you. And besides, I was feeling . . . well, pretty obligated to her. We haven't been going together that long, but things got kind of intense between us." He flushed a bright red. "I guess I haven't had a lot of experience with girls, and the physical stuff . . . well, it sort of got out of hand before I knew what was happening." He gave me an inquiring look, as if to ask whether I understood, and I nodded.

"I mean, I really like Annie a lot," he continued. "But after I met you, I realized I wasn't in love with her. I began to feel pretty dishonest. And disloyal— to Annie, I mean. And to myself. So I decided to cool it, avoid you at school and hope that my feelings would change. I was so sure that they would. But it didn't happen. Instead—"

Somebody tapped on the closed window and we both jumped. A guy wearing a yellow slicker was standing outside in the rain, holding our order. It was Mitch. He gave me a surprised grin, as he if he'd expected to see me with David rather than Josh. Josh rolled down the window, paid Mitch, and took our milk shakes, handing one to me.

"Instead, every time I saw you, my feelings got stronger," he went on after Mitch had left. "The trouble was . . ." He looked up, his eyes on mine, and I could tell he was searching for the right words. "The trouble was David. I . . . well, I was getting pretty jealous of him. And then, that night at Annie's house, I had to sit there and know that he was the one who was kissing you. I knew I didn't have the right to feel jealous. David's a nice guy. I could see why you'd like him. But I couldn't help it."

I took a sip of my milk shake, but I couldn't taste it. I couldn't believe that all these weeks Josh had been feeling exactly the way *I'd* felt.

Josh chuckled wryly. "Feeling dishonest is bad enough. I don't want to hurt anyone. But after last night I had to be honest with you. And with myself." He leaned back in the seat, looking relieved. "Well, that's over. I've confessed. And I won't blame you if you get angry or slap me or something."

I looked at him, my heart still pounding. "I told you before, I'm not angry," I whispered, moving closer to him. "You said all there is to say . . . for both of us."

"What?" He sat up straight and looked at me intently. "Did you say what I think you said? Are you saying that—"

"That I care for you? Yes," I said, my pulse racing. "All those things that were going on inside you . . . they were my feelings, too. The same thing was happening to me."

Josh leaned forward. He quickly set both our milk shakes on the floor. Then his arms closed around me, and his mouth covered mine. He pulled me against him, and I responded automatically to his kiss. His arms around me were like fire, and I was softening to his touch, melting into him—

Somebody was banging on the window. Josh pulled away a little, his lips against my cheek. He was breathing heavily.

"Hey, Lauren," a familiar voice yelled, "is that you?"

It was Maggie.

"Hey, Lauren!" Maggie yelled again, pounding on the window. "Let me in. It's raining out here!"

"It's Maggie," I explained with a sigh. "My stepsister."

Josh rolled his eyes at me. Leaning over me, he opened the door. "Climb in," he invited, forcing a laugh.

Maggie hoisted herself into the front seat, dripping raincoat, muddy boots, and all. "I thought it was you, Lauren," she said to me. "I was taking the shortcut home from Suzie's house, through the parking lot, and it was wet. When I saw you, I thought maybe you'd give me a ride." She noticed our milk shakes on the floor. "Hey, can I have some of that?" As she leaned forward to grab one, she looked at Josh. "Hey, I know who you are! You're Annie's boyfriend. I saw you at the balloon races."

Josh nodded. "I remember you, too."

"Are you Lauren's boyfriend, too?" Without waiting for an answer, Maggie added, "I saw you kissing her." She made a face. "Gooey gush."

"Her favorite phrase," I said to Josh. Turning to Maggie, I snapped, "You shouldn't go around spying through people's car windows."

Maggie didn't pay any attention to me. "Well, *are* you?" she demanded again. "Lauren's boyfriend, I mean."

I bit my lip, wishing she would shut up and go away.

Josh looked at me, and there was a hint of amusement in his eyes.

"How can you have two different girlfriends at once?"

"Maggie!" I said, embarrassed—and troubled, too. It wasn't a question that either of us could answer just now.

She finished the last of my milk shake with a loud slurp, and announced, "Well, I'm never going to have a boyfriend. Boys are stupid."

"That's good," I observed dryly, "because I doubt if you'll ever get one."

Josh laughed and started the truck. "Just wait a few years, Maggie," he told her. "You might change your mind."

In a few minutes Josh had pulled into Carolyn's driveway, and Maggie slid out into the rain. "Aren't you coming in?" she asked.

"In a minute," I said. I watched her go as far as the porch, where she sat down on the porch swing. I rolled down the truck window. "Stop spying!" I yelled. "Go inside. And stay away from the the windows."

Making a face at me, Maggie flounced into the house.

"Some kid," Josh said.

"That's what my father says," I replied through clenched teeth. "Me, I'd like to strangle her."

Josh shifted on the seat. "Well, she's right about one thing," he said. "A guy can't have two girlfriends at once, at least not in Vermilion." He grinned ruefully. "So, I guess the big question is, what do we do now? Do we tell Annie and David, before this thing goes any further?"

I looked down. Josh's idea was a good one—probably the *right* one. But I was so happy right now. I didn't want to have to think about the confrontation there would be with Annie, or the pain and unhappiness that were certain to follow. Right then I just wanted to have Josh to myself, to spend a little time reveling in the thought that he returned my affection, that he loved me as much as I loved him.

"Do we have to tell anybody right away?" I asked. "Can't we wait? I'd like to just be happy for a few days."

He picked up my hand and kissed each of my fingertips gently. "Maybe you're right," he said. "Maybe it would be a good idea to let things settle down a little. But I don't think we ought to wait too long. I don't feel right about deceiving Annie." His wide mouth spread into a grin. "And besides, I want to be able to be able to kiss you in public, without worrying about who's looking."

He glanced toward the front window of our house. There sat Maggie, with her nose pressed against the glass.

"You're looking very happy, Lauren," Dad said, as I passed him the lasagna at dinner that night.

"It's because she's got a new boyfriend," Maggie told them importantly. "She and Annie have the same boyfriend. His name is Josh."

Dad raised an eyebrow. "Living dangerously?" he asked with a grin.

Carolyn gave Maggie a second piece of garlic bread. "Don't gossip about people's private lives, dear."

"It's not gossip, it's true," Maggie protested. "I saw Josh kissing Lauren this afternoon." She took a piece of bread and began rolling it into a little ball.

I felt myself coloring, but at least they didn't seem to be taking Maggie seriously. At that minute Maggie's grandmother telephoned to say hello, and by the time Maggie got back from talking on the phone, the conversation had turned to other things, and Maggie had forgotten all about Josh.

At least for the moment.

7

I SAW JOSH ON MONDAY MORNING BEFORE SCHOOL, and we walked to homeroom together. I felt wonderful walking beside him. But Josh looked uncomfortable.

"I've been thinking," he said. "Maybe it isn't such a good idea to put off telling Annie. I'd sure hate it if she found out about us by accident. I'll feel better when everything's out in the open. What do you think we should do, Lauren?"

"We?" I asked. I'd been pushing the thought of Annie out of my mind. "Do you mean we ought to do it together?"

"I don't know," Josh said.

"I don't know, either. Can't we postpone talking about it for just a couple of days longer?" I pleaded. I didn't want to face the unpleasantness that was bound to follow our confession. I didn't want anything to spoil my happiness. "A few more days won't make any difference, will it?"

"I guess not," Josh agreed reluctantly. "To tell

the truth, it's not something I'm exactly looking forward to, either."

We joined the kids going into homeroom. In the crowd he touched my hand, and his touch, warm and tingling, stayed with me all day long.

If nobody else noticed that I was looking unusually happy, Annie did. She bugged me with questions all day long, but I was evasive. On the way home from school that afternoon, she announced triumphantly that she finally had it figured out.

"You've got what figured out?" I asked nervously.

"You're in love!" she said.

I stared at her. I stopped breathing. Was I as obvious as all that? Had she guessed?

"Come on, Lauren, don't play games with me," she said, swinging her book bag from one shoulder to the other. "You're acting exactly like you're in love." Before I could say anything, she asked, "Does David feel the same way?"

I started breathing again. For an instant I was tempted to tell her the truth, but I just smiled in a mysterious way, and that seemed to satisfy her.

"I'm really glad for you, Lauren," she said. "For both of you. David is a very nice guy. He deserves someone like you."

"Uh, yes, he's pretty terrific," I agreed uncomfortably. As I said it, all I could hear was Josh saying, "David's a nice guy. . . . I don't want to hurt anyone." How could we be doing this to our friends? I didn't want to hurt Annie, either. But suddenly I knew she was going to get hurt. I couldn't pretend any longer that it was just Josh and me, alone together. There was Annie to consider, and David.

"Uh, Annie," I began. "I—" I stopped and swallowed. What could I say? But I had to tell her. "Annie, I—"

She wasn't listening. "I've got some pretty big news for you, too," she said.

I gave up. I simply didn't have the courage to tell her. "What is it?" I asked.

"I got elected to be in the Queen's Court at the Harvest Festival! I just found out this afternoon."

"The court? Annie, that's great!"

It *was* big news. The Harvest Festival was the most important school dance of the year and would take place three weeks from the coming Friday. The three most popular girls from each class got elected to the Queen's Court. Annie had explained all that to me when we'd voted for the court last week.

I grinned at her. "What are the chances you'll be elected queen?"

"Well, there are twelve of us in the court, so I guess the chances are one in twelve. Probably better than that, since I'm a senior, and the queen is usually a senior."

"Maybe one in three?" I asked.

"Maybe." Her green eyes were shining. "Oh, Lauren, wouldn't it be terrific if I won? Just think, Josh would be king, and we'd get to ride through town on the festival float and sit on the thrones at the dance. And we'd get our pictures in the newspaper and in the yearbook."

I cleared my throat. "Josh . . . would be king?"

"Sure. That's the way it works. The queen's date is always crowned king. He wears a tux and sits on a throne. I'll bet Josh will look absolutely terrific in a tux. We'll be the perfect couple. Don't you think so?"

I hesitated. "Yes," I said finally. My voice was flat. "The perfect couple."

I felt like a first-class jerk, keeping up the routine, but I didn't know what else I could do.

On Tuesday I was having lunch with David, as usual. I knew it wasn't exactly fair to him, but as long as I stuck with David, people probably wouldn't think I was seriously interested in Josh. Breaking it off with him would mean that I had to give him some kind of explanation. I couldn't tell him the truth; he might turn around and tell Annie. But what *could* I tell him? I was trying to think of something when he broke into my thoughts.

"Annie said something interesting in homeroom this morning," he told me.

I took a bite of my salad. "She did?"

"Yes." David looked meaningfully at me. "She said, 'Congratulations.' "

"For what?"

"That's what I wanted to know. So I asked her. And you know what she told me? She said, 'For you and Lauren. I think the two of you make a great couple.' And then she looked as though she was afraid she'd said too much, and I couldn't get anything more out of her."

"Oh," I said. What else could I say? I wished I hadn't let Annie believe that I cared about David, but I had, and now I was locked into the lie. For the first time ever I was truly in love, and yet things in my life just kept going from bad to worse.

David put his hand over mine on the table. "Annie didn't say so," he said, "but I got the idea that maybe you'd told her that you . . . that you liked me. A lot. And she thought that we'd talked it over, so I was in on the secret, too."

I put down my fork, trying to think of a way to head this off. How could I stop David from getting the wrong idea? But he *already* had the wrong idea. I was too late. He was pressing on.

"I mean, I know that you two are best friends. You probably talk a lot, about guys. . . ." He paused, his brown eyes very serious. "I mean, if you did tell her, Lauren, I wish you'd tell me, too." He paused again, and added, much more softly, "Because I like you, very much."

"I . . . I like you, too, David," I said hesitantly. Before I had the chance to add, "but not in the way you mean," we were interrupted. One of the school cheerleaders had come over to our table. She was carrying a clipboard and writing people's names on it.

"Hey, you guys want to sign up for the bus for the game Friday night?"

"The bus?" I asked.

"Sure," David said. "The game is at Hoopeston, about forty miles away. The school sends a couple of buses for the fans. Instead of driving cars to the game, a lot of kids ride the bus. Why don't we go? It's a lot of fun, actually. Sort of like a traveling pep rally."

I wasn't sure I wanted to go to the game with

David, but if I said no, I'd have to give a reason, and I couldn't think of a single one. I said yes. David put both our names down on the sign-up sheet, and the cheerleader left.

"Listen," David said, leaning forward, "about what we were talking about, I'm really glad to know how you feel." His eyes were warm, and he was smiling.

"But—" I stopped. I knew what I ought to say. I ought to say, "David, I like you very much as a friend, but I don't feel romantic about you." But the warm, trusting, look on his face stopped me.

"But what?"

I shook my head. "Nothing," I said, feeling like a total liar.

If I felt bad then, it only got worse later.

I was at my locker after school that afternoon, getting my homework together, when Josh stepped out of the crowd. My heart did its usual quick back flip.

"Hey," he said, sounding troubled, "I saw your name with David's on the sign-up sheet for the bus Friday night. Are you going to the game with him?"

I nodded.

His voice was low and tense. "I was hoping that maybe you and I would be able to arrange it so we could go to the game together."

"I don't see how we could do that." I looked over my shoulder to make sure that nobody could overhear us. "We'd have to tell Annie about us right away. And you heard the news, I suppose, about her being elected to the Queen's Court for the Harvest Festival."

"Yeah. She called me last night to tell me. She was pretty excited about the idea of riding the float and getting her picture taken and maybe even being queen."

"Well, when we talked about it, what she was most thrilled about was the idea of your being king." I paused. "It means a lot to her, Josh."

"Are you saying—?" He kicked the toe of his sneaker against the lockers. "Lauren, the festival is three weeks from Friday. *Three whole weeks!*"

I put my French book in my bag, not looking at him. "I know."

"We can't wait that long! *I* can't wait that long! I want to—"

"I think we have to wait," I broke in, "unless you've got a better—"

"Hi, you guys," a bright voice rang out behind us. Neither of us had seen Annie come up.

I gave a guilty start, and Josh's ears turned red. "Hi," we said in unison. I'm sure we looked terribly guilty, but Annie didn't seem to notice. In fact, she seemed preoccupied.

Putting a hand on my arm, she said, "Listen, Lauren, I've been feeling awful about something that happened this morning, and I want to apologize."

I couldn't look at Josh. "For what?" I asked.

She opened her locker and shoved her books in. "I think I said something to David that I shouldn't have."

"To David?" I asked, not thinking. Then I realized what she was talking about, but she was already explaining.

"Well," Annie said, "I said, 'Congratulations,' and he pretended not to know what I was talking about, so I didn't say any more." She eyed me curiously. "I hope I didn't mess anything up, Lauren. I didn't know that you and David were trying to make a big secret out of it."

I could feel Josh's eyes on me.

"Congratulations for what?" he asked.

How was I going to explain? I couldn't really, until we got a chance to talk in private.

"It's okay, Annie," I said, ignoring Josh's questions. "You didn't mess anything up."

"Trying to make a big secret out of *what*?" Josh persisted, sounding puzzled.

"I can't tell." With a tantalizing grin, Annie put her arm through his. Winking at me, she added, "My lips are sealed. You'll have to ask Lauren—or David. It's their secret."

"I see." Josh gave me a scrutinizing look.

What had I gotten myself into?

Annie unwittingly came to my rescue. "Hey, Josh, enough of secrets! How about taking the two prettiest girls in the class to Randy's for ice cream?"

Josh glanced quickly at me, then down at his watch. "Oops, sorry," he said. "I've got to go interview a couple of football players for a newspaper story."

I was sure he was inventing a reason not to go with the two of us. I didn't blame him. He probably felt every bit as uncomfortable as I did.

Annie dropped Josh's arm and took mine, giving

him a teasing, make-believe pout. "Well, be that way, if you want to. Lauren and I will go without you. We'll have a good, long, girls' talk. We'll talk about you. And David. Won't we, Lauren?"

I pulled my arm away, then hugged her quickly, feeling remorseful. "Sorry, Annie, but I can't. Not tonight. I . . . promised Carolyn I'd be home right after school to . . . to help her with some chores."

Annie looked downcast, and I felt even guiltier. I wished I could have gone with her. It would have been nice to have one of our old, silly, talks. I wanted things to be normal again, the way they'd been before Josh came into the picture. I wanted to chatter on about dates and boys and clothes and what we were going to be when we grew up. But we couldn't talk about those things anymore, because I had a secret. And when Annie found out what it was, she'd probably never want to talk to me again.

Josh called that night, and I tried to explain what had happened with David. He seemed to understand, but I could tell that he wasn't happy about the situation. He argued that we couldn't wait three and a half weeks before we told Annie about us, and I said that it wasn't right for her to have to find somebody else to take her to the Harvest Festival. When we said good-bye, nothing had been settled. We'd just been talking around in circles.

The telephone was in the upstairs hallway. I'd just hung up and was sitting there with my back to the wall, feeling pretty hopeless, when Maggie stuck her head around the banister.

"So, he's trying to get rid of your cousin, huh?" she asked with mischievous, bright-eyed interest. "He doesn't want to have two girlfriends after all?"

I jumped up. "Have you been listening?" It was a dumb question. Of course she'd been listening. I stormed downstairs and into the kitchen, where Carolyn was making brownies for a bake sale that Maggie's class was having the next day.

"This has got to stop," I yelled.

Carolyn looked up. "What's got to stop?"

"Maggie's been spying on my phone conversations. I don't have any privacy around here! And don't tell me I need a sense of humor," I added in a quieter voice. "You wouldn't think it was very funny if I listened in on *your* conversations."

"You're right," Carolyn said, scraping the bowl. "You should have your own telephone. Your dad and I were talking about it this weekend. What color would you like?"

I stared at her, surprised. "White, I guess," I replied.

"Good. That's what I'll order," she said. "And send Maggie down here to me. I have a word or two to say to that child!"

I was on my way out of the kitchen when she added, "Oh, by the way, Lauren, your dad and I are taking Maggie to the Vermilion High football game in Hoopeston on Friday night. Would you like to come with us?"

"Thanks," I said, "but I'm going on the bus." I stamped out of the kitchen. But I didn't stamp very hard. At least she was going to lecture Maggie. And I was going to get my own phone.

* * *

David had been right. The ride to Hoopeston on the school bus was a traveling pep rally, with cheers and songs and lots of yelling. David got on the bus first and took a seat for us in the very back. After a while I understood why. Several couples in front of us had dropped out of the cheering and were taking advantage of the darkness to make out.

Josh and Annie were one of those couples. I couldn't tell, in the dark, whether Josh was kissing her or letting her kiss him. But whatever way it was, it hurt, and a wave of hot jealousy came over me. I couldn't get up and leave, the way I had that night at Annie's house, so when David put his arms around me and pulled me close, I buried my face in his shoulder so that I didn't have to look at Josh and Annie. And when he began to kiss me, I kissed him back, half out of jealous spite at the way Josh was acting. I felt like a jerk, using David that way, but I couldn't help myself. It was awful.

The football game was an exciting one, but I didn't really see much of it. When we sat down in the bleachers, Josh arranged it so that he and I were sitting next to each other, with David and Annie on the outside.

The September evening was chilly, and the sky threatened rain, so we spread a couple of blankets over our legs. As the first play began, Josh's hand groped for mine under the blankets. His fingers curled around mine, and our hands rested on my thigh. I could feel his warmth through my jeans, and the excitement of being next to him made me grin with a happy giddiness. Being so close to Josh made it hard to concentrate on the action on the field, even though David, on other side, was giving me a play-by-play commentary on the game. And I had to pretend to be interested. Every now and then he would put his arm around me and squeeze my shoulders. I could tell that he was having a good time because he thought that I was with him, and I felt horrible about it—and deceitful. Every second I was afraid that the blanket might get jerked away and everyone would see that Josh and I were holding hands.

As if things weren't bad enough, Dad and Carolyn and Maggie arrived after the game got started. Out of an entire row of bleachers, they managed to take seats right behind us. I'd forgotten that they were coming to the game, and my surprise when I saw them was more like sick dismay. Suddenly my stomach was churning. I exchanged a worried look with Josh, and I could tell we were both thinking the same thing: What if Maggie deliberately said something about Josh and me in front of Annie and David?

All through the first half of the game I sat hunched over miserably, with Josh holding my hand under the blanket, David's arm around my shoulders, and Maggie's bony knees digging into my back. How had things gotten to this point? Everything had always been so steady and predictable before I met Josh. Then it was chilling and scary and exciting and terrible all at once. My worst fears were realized at halftime, when Dad and Carolyn got up to go to the refreshment stand, leaving Maggie behind.

"Hey," she said loudly. "You've got two girl-friends. How come?"

I panicked. Trying to shut Maggie up would only make things worse. She might tell what she'd seen last Saturday at the Burger-Shake Drive-In.

"What are you talking about?" David asked, before I could say a word.

For a second Josh looked as uncomfortable as I felt, and his blue eyes shifted from Annie to me to David. Then he seemed to pull himself into control. Half-turning on the bleacher bench, he gave Maggie a teasing grin. He pulled his hand out from under the blanket and put one arm around Annie, the other around me. "Why have I got two girl-friends? Because I'm lucky, I guess. How many boyfriends have you got, Maggie? A couple of dozen?"

Maggie made a face. "Boys, yuck," she said.

Josh leaned back and whispered something to Maggie. She smiled from ear to ear and nodded. "Which would you rather have," he asked, standing up, "popcorn or peanuts?"

"Popcorn," she said quickly. Then, changing her mind, "No, peanuts."

"Peanuts it is," Josh agreed. He glanced at me. "Want anything?"

I stood up. "I'll go, too," I said. "I need to stretch."

"I'll save your seats," Maggie announced importantly.

David and Annie decided to come along, so all

four of us headed off toward the refreshment stand. Once there, Annie got involved in a conversation with Tina Helprin, one of the other two seniors elected to the Queen's Court, and David took off for the rest room.

Josh gave a quick glance around, then pulled me off to the side, into a dark corner behind the refreshment stand. "This isn't exactly fun, you know," he said in a low voice. "First the bus ride, and now Maggie."

I sighed. "Do you think it's fun for me? Who knows what she'll say next?"

"It's not really Maggie I'm so worried about," Josh said. He put his fingers under my chin and raised my face so I had to meet his gaze. His blue eyes had darkened, and they seemed almost black. I'd never seen him look so serious. "The fact is, I hate seeing you with David. Do you have to let him kiss you?"

I took a deep breath. I felt like crying—or laughing. I wasn't sure which.

"But you were kissing Annie," I said defensively, pulling back. "What's the difference?"

Josh softened a little. "I'm sorry, Lauren. That was stupid. I apologize." He pulled me into his arms again and held me close, resting his lips against my forehead. Then his mouth was on mine and he was kissing me, pulling me against him as if he couldn't hold me close enough. I held him just as tight, and kissed him feverishly.

"Oh, Lauren," he said with a groan, pulling away. "We can't go on this way. I want to kiss you and hold you without being afraid that somebody's

going to find out about us. I want to let everyone
know how I feel about you."

"I know, Josh," I whispered. "I want that, too."

At that moment there was a loud crash from
inside the refreshment stand, and I jumped as I
remembered where we were. I quickly pulled
away, looking frantically around us. "Josh, somebody might *see* us."

He shook his head, and his gaze followed mine
around the concessions area. Neither Annie nor
David was in sight. "You're right," he said. "I know
we shouldn't be doing this. But we *have* to be together, Lauren. We've got to figure out what to do.
We have to talk, and not over the phone, either.
It's got to be someplace where we won't be dis-
turbed."

"Where? When?" I didn't want to sneak around
behind Annie's back, but he was right—we had to
talk.

We stepped out into the light and got in line.
"How about if you come out to the hangar tomorrow afternoon?" Josh asked in a low voice.

"Okay," I said. "Annie's going to Springfield to
shop for a dress for the Harvest Festival."

Josh groaned and stuck his hands in his pockets.
"The Harvest Festival. Don't remind me."

"What's so bad about the Harvest Festival?" Annie asked, coming up behind us.

Josh turned bright red. "It's just that . . ." His
voice trailed off.

"Josh was just saying," I put in quickly, "that
he's not especially wild about the idea of wearing
a tux and riding the float. He's afraid some of his

friends will throw eggs at him." I was surprised at how quickly the lie slipped out. What was happening to me, that I could lie to my best friend this way?

Annie laughed and tucked her hand into his. "That's okay, Josh," she said. "Maybe it won't happen. Maybe I won't get elected queen after all. Then you won't have to be king." She stood on tiptoe and kissed the tip of his ear. "Unfortunately, we won't know until the day of the dance. And that's three whole weeks away. I can hardly wait, can you?"

Josh and I exchanged glances.

"No," he said quietly. "I can't wait."

8

THE PHONE RANG JUST BEFORE NINE THE NEXT MORN-
ing. When Carolyn called from downstairs that it
was for me, I took it on my telephone, which had
just been installed the day before.

"Hi," came Annie's voice over the line. "Listen,
I've got this great idea. I'm going to have a surprise
birthday party for Josh."

"Uh . . . when is his birthday?"

"The week after the Harvest Festival. We can
have a barbecue and a hayride. Dad says he'll get
us a tractor and wagon. I'm going to start inviting
people right away."

"The week after the Harvest Festival?" That
meant *another* week before Josh and I could tell
her about us.

Before I could say anything else, Annie was on
to another subject. "Do you want to go shopping
in Springfield with Mom and me today?"

"I . . . I can't," I said. I hadn't expected her to
ask me. "I promised Carolyn that if—if it was a

96

warm day, I'd surprise Maggie by taking her hiking."

It was a lie, pure and simple, but I couldn't tell Annie that I had a date with her boyfriend. At least, thank heaven, it was a safe lie. Now that I had my own phone, I had the privacy of talking in my room, where Maggie couldn't hear me.

Or could she? Just then, there was a distinct click on the line. "Hang on a minute, Annie," I said. I hurried to the door and opened it a crack. Sure enough, Maggie was tiptoeing away from the hall phone. I gave her a black look and slammed the door.

"What was that all about?" Annie asked curiously when I got back to the phone.

"Oh, nothing," I said. "Listen, I'm sorry I can't go to Springfield. Have a good time, huh?"

"Yeah, I will. Listen, what do you think about white?"

"White?"

"A white dress," Annie said. "For the Harvest Festival. I've been thinking about the color I want, and I was thinking either green or white." She laughed a little self-consciously. "White might be better for a queen, don't you think?"

I pressed my lips together. "Yes, white would be good."

"On the other hand," she went on, sounding excited, "green is a nice color for me, don't you think? The right green, that is—sort of an emerald, maybe."

"Uh-huh." I wasn't thinking about dresses. I was

thinking about Maggie and what I was going to say to her as soon as I got off the phone.

"So, maybe I'll look for green," she concluded. "Something off-the-shoulder. But no ruffles. I hate ruffles." She paused. "Anyway, Mom said that if we don't find anything in Springfield, next week we can drive to Chicago."

"Great."

"Well, if I find a dress I like, I'll bring it over and show it to you tonight. If I don't, you can go to Chicago with us next weekend. Okay?"

"Okay," I told her. "Sure. Great."

I wanted to get off the phone, but Annie seemed reluctant to hang up. "Why don't I come over tonight, even if I don't find a dress," she suggested. Her voice sounded a little forced, almost as if she were worried about something. "Josh is going to be busy with some family thing, and, I don't know, I guess I don't really want to spend Saturday night by myself. Do you have plans with David?"

"No," I answered unsteadily. "Come on over. It'll be fun. Um . . . is everything okay, Annie?"

"Yes—I mean, I guess so. Josh seemed kind of distant all week. It's not like him not to want to spend a weekend night together." She was talking in a rush, not really giving me a chance to comment. "But with school starting and everything, I guess it's natural that we're both busier."

"Yeah," I said. I knew the real reason why Josh was suddenly backing off from Annie, and I didn't trust myself to say anything else.

"Listen, thanks for all your help," Annie said. "I

knew that if I talked to you, you'd have some good ideas. See you later. Bye."

After we'd hung up, I marched straight to Maggie's room. She was getting her hiking shoes out of her closet.

"You can put those away," I said.

"But I thought we were going—I mean . . ."

"You were listening on the other phone."

Maggie lifted her chin. "So what if I was? You can't do a thing about it."

"Who says?" I retorted, turning for the door. "I'm going to go right downstairs and tell Carolyn."

"No, you won't." Maggie gave me a wicked grin. "Because if you do, I'll tell Annie that I saw you kissing her boyfriend."

I clenched my fists. "You wouldn't dare!" I hissed.

"Want to bet?" Maggie inquired sweetly. "And I think you were telling her a lie just now, too. You weren't planning to take me hiking today, were you? I bet you're going to spend the afternoon with Josh, aren't you?"

I was trapped. Maggie looked so smug, I wanted to strangle her.

"That's okay," she went on. "If you won't tell Mom about me eavesdropping, I won't tell Annie that you're cheating on her. Or that you lied." She tossed her hiking shoes back into the closet. "And I won't even make you take me hiking," she added generously.

I walked out and slammed the door. Behind me I could hear Maggie chanting, in an infuriating sing-songy voice, "Lauren's mad, and I'm glad."

Carolyn was standing at the top of the stairs. Throwing a quick glance at Maggie's closed door, she said, "I hate to ask, but what was all that about, Lauren?"

"You have a problem daughter," I said between clenched teeth.

But even though I was furious at Maggie, I knew she was right. To put it bluntly, Carolyn had *two* problem daughters—one who eavesdropped and another who cheated on her best friend. And I had the terrible feeling that my crime was a whole lot worse than Maggie's. Maggie was only annoying. But I was going to cause Annie a great deal of pain. What gave me the right to hurt her so?

But Carolyn couldn't know any of that. Her shoulders were drooped, and she looked discouraged. "Maggie just isn't adjusting the way I hoped she would," she confided. "She's terribly unhappy. Sometimes I think maybe I shouldn't have put my happiness before hers—marrying your father, I mean. Her life would have been easier if things had stayed the way they were—just the two of us." She paused. "If you've got any ideas about how to deal with this, Lauren, I'd certainly be glad to hear them."

Carolyn looked so upset that for a fleeting instant I felt like putting my arms around her to comfort her. But I couldn't. *I* was the one who needed comforting. And as far as ideas were concerned, I didn't have any, about Maggie or anything else. With a shake of my head, I went into my room and closed the door. A wave of despair washed over me.

Everything had gone wrong in my life, and it had all begun when my father and Carolyn had put their happiness first. His marriage had forced me into a new way of life and into a new family I didn't want to belong to. I didn't need another mother, and I certainly didn't want a bratty little stepsister.

But those were all minor problems, sort of like little thunderstorms, compared to the tornado that was ruining my life. If I were honest, I'd have to admit that I'd caused most of my trouble myself. I'd let myself get involved with David. It was my fault he thought I cared for him more than I did. I'd let myself fall in love with my best friend's boy-friend, and whatever I did was going to hurt her. And worst of all, I was about to do something I knew was wrong. I had agreed to meet Josh behind Annie's back, and I'd compounded my guilt by lying to her.

But one thing came shining through all the turmoil and darkness inside me, like a bright, clear, beacon. That was the knowledge that I loved Josh. Whatever else lay ahead—for Annie, for Josh, for David, and me—that love was still bright and untarnished.

9

I'M GOING TO MEET JOSH; I'M GOING TO SEE JOSH. THE words were a song in my heart as I drove Dad's car swiftly along the highway toward the airport. I made up my mind to concentrate on the love I felt for him and set aside my guilt. Right then it was easier to forget about Annie and David, for I was full of wild anticipation. In a few moments I would be in Josh's arms, and the thought made me breathless.

At the terminal, Jumbo was eating a giant ham sandwich. "You lookin' for Josh?" he asked, as if out of habit. He squinted at me. "You ain't the same girl who comes here all the time," he remarked. "You ain't got red hair."

"No," I said, blushing. "But I am looking for Josh. Is he at the hangar?"

"Last I saw." Jumbo went back to his ham sandwich.

I went across the concrete apron and paused beside the white Cessna with the wide blue stripe down the side. Had it only been a few weeks since I'd flown in it? Only a few weeks since I'd seen Josh for the first time? So much had happened that it seemed like months, a year, forever. I rested my hand on the wing.

The concrete in front of the hangar was empty, so I stepped inside. It was much cooler here, out of the sun. Off to the left, in the shadows, I glimpsed an antique-looking airplane painted greenish-brown, with red, white, and blue stripes on the tail. Then I saw him. He was off to the right, in a brightly lit area hung with tools and airplane parts, bent over a cluttered workbench. He was wearing a flannel shirt, and his hands were covered with grease. I stood for a few minutes studying his profile, admiring the deft, sure, way he worked, the intent frown on his face, his total absorption in his work. When he reached up to brush the dark hair out of his eyes, I caught my breath.

Then he looked up and saw me. I could hardly breathe as he came toward me with quick, eager, strides, holding out his arms. But when he'd almost reached me, he noticed the crisp white jeans and top I'd worn. Glancing down at his grimy hands, he made a comic face. "Maybe I'd better wash before I touch," he said.

"Put your hands behind your back," I ordered, and leaned toward him. He kissed me, gently at first, and then more deeply. After a long moment he stepped back, pulling in his breath.

"I can't kiss you the way I want to if I can't hold you," he said.

He turned abruptly to wash his hands in a corner sink while I wandered over to the old plane.

After a minute Josh came to join me. "What do you think of Jenny?"

"Jenny?" I was hardly listening, concentrating instead on the way his lips moved when he talked.

He gestured toward the old greenish-brown plane. It had two wings, one on top of the other, tied together with rods and wires. It only had front wheels, so that the tail dragged on the ground, and it looked awfully flimsy. I wondered if it would actually fly.

"This is a Curtiss JN-4. Back in the old days everybody called her a Jenny."

"It . . . she's very interesting," I said. "Is it polite to ask her age?"

Josh chuckled. "She doesn't mind," he said, affection in his voice. "She's proud of her years. The Jennies were used as trainers during World War One, and after the war as barnstormers." I looked at him questioningly, and he explained. "A pilot would fly his Jenny from town to town, taking people for rides and doing stunts, like wing walking. The planes were even used in the movies. Dad and I found this one in a barn in Indiana, under a pile of hay."

I stared at the plane, trying to imagine somebody walking on the narrow wings. "But how can you land it?" I asked. "It doesn't have any wheels in the back."

"The Jennies were designed to land and take off on grass," Josh said. He put his hand on the wing. "She'll be ready to fly again in just a couple of weeks," he added. "Dad and I are going to race her at the Antique Air Show." He pointed at the fuselage. "See? She's got two cockpits—one in the back for the pilot, one in front for the navigator."

"You mean this rickety thing still flies?" I ran my finger down the wing, which seemed to be made out of canvas, covered with paint.

"You bet she still flies," Josh said proudly. "Flies like a bird. I've been working on her all summer, and I'm really eager to see how we do in the competition." He turned me around to face him and gently stroked my cheek. "We can talk about airplanes later, though," he said. "Right now I just want to kiss you. Okay?"

"Are you asking my permission?" I whispered.

His blue eyes were shimmering and intense as they searched mine. He pulled me toward an old automobile seat in the corner that served as a sofa, its leather cracked and worn. There was a stack of airplane magazines on it. Pushing them onto the floor, he dusted the seat off and pulled me down onto it beside him.

"Not really," he said. Then his lips were on mine, and I forgot everything but the electric warmth of his body against mine and the circle of his strong arms around me. I could feel his heart beating, his breath coming faster, in time with my own.

After a while we pulled apart, and he sat back, his eyes on mine, his hands still on my shoulders. "I've never felt like this before, Lauren," he said. "About anyone."

I shivered. "Not even about Annie," I whispered, "in the beginning?"

He shook his head. "No, not even about her. She's a great girl, and I really like being around her. But after I met you, I realized she and I were just . . . well, I mean—" He dropped his hands. "We were just two people having fun together."

"But you've been more than that to her," I reminded him. "You've been the first big romance in her life." For an instant I could almost feel the pain Annie was going to feel when she found out the truth.

"I know that. Believe me, I know," Josh answered. His voice was sad. "That's why I've got to tell her that I'm not in love with her, that I care for somebody else. And the sooner the better, as far as I'm concerned. I'd hate for her to hear about it from somebody else."

I sighed. "There's something I guess I'd better tell you," I said. I filled him in on what had happened with Maggie that morning, and the threat she had made. "If Maggie wants to cause trouble," I added, "she can certainly do it."

Josh nodded. "That's a good reason for us to tell Annie right away," he said firmly. "Like tonight. Before Maggie blows the whistle."

I bit my lip. "But what about the Harvest Festival? It means so much to her. And there's something else, too." The party was supposed to be a surprise, but I had to tell him. "She's going to give a party on your birthday. She's already making plans for a barbecue and a hayride. She's starting to invite people."

"Oh, God." Josh groaned. "That means another whole week!"

"This is getting more complicated all the time," I said.

"You know," he said, "there'll always be a reason not to tell her." He reached for me and held me close against him. "I can't keep us a secret for a whole month! If Maggie doesn't let the cat out of the bag, somebody's going to guess it just from the way I look at you. And there's David," he added soberly.

"I know," I said with a sigh. "I'm not being fair to him. I . . . I have to let him know that I don't care for him, at least not the way he wants me to. I'm not going out with him again."

"When will you tell him?" Josh asked.

"The next time I see him."

He leaned forward and kissed the tip of my nose, the corner of my mouth, my lips. "Then let me tell Annie," he whispered.

I pushed him away and sat upright.

"We have to," he said urgently. "Let me tell her tonight, before she invites a lot of people to the party. While she's still got time to find another date for the Harvest Festival." His face twisted into a grimace. "I don't know how much more of this I can stand, Lauren. I want you all the time, but every time I touch you, I feel like a sneak."

The tears swelled in my eyes. "I . . . know," I said. He was right, and I knew it. We had to tell her. But not yet. Not just yet. "After the party," I insisted. "Please, Josh, it's only a few weeks."

There was a long silence. "I guess," he eventually said, sighing. Then he traced my lips with his finger. "But I want you to know that, whatever happens, I love you. And loving you is the best thing I've ever done in my life."

10

It was well after four by the time I got home. Coming in the back door, I found Carolyn sitting alone at the kitchen table. She'd been potting plants, and her hands were still stained with dirt. The kitchen counter was loaded with yellow mums, and there was a big bowlful of the cheerful yellow flowers in the middle of the table. Carolyn's hands were wrapped around a cup of hot tea, and she looked worried.

Still glowing from having been with Josh, I said hello and poured a cup for myself. I was about to take it upstairs, but Carolyn stopped me.

"Could we talk for a minute, Lauren?" she asked. "I need some advice."

I sat down and looked at her, only half paying attention.

"Maggie and I had a talk after you left," Carolyn said. She turned the cup in her fingers. "She says she wants to go to Springfield and live with her grandmother."

"Her grandmother?" I stared at her. "But why?"
I didn't need to ask. I already knew the answer.

"Because she's unhappy," Carolyn replied. "Because she doesn't feel that we . . . that I love her.
Because she doesn't want to be a member of this
family." She dropped her face into her hands.

It was so quiet that I could hear the clock ticking
on the wall. I stared at Carolyn, her shoulders thin
and vulnerable under her green T-shirt. This morning I'd wanted to comfort her and couldn't. I'd felt
that I was the one who needed comforting. Now,
after being with Josh, I felt differently.

"I'm sorry," I said. I got up and stood behind her
chair, putting my arms around her and laying my
cheek against her hair. "I'm really sorry, Carolyn."

After a moment I realized that she was crying.
"It'll be okay," I said softly.

"Maybe it won't be okay," Carolyn said. "I'm not
sure anymore." She blew her nose into a paper
napkin. "Sometimes I really feel cornered, Lauren.
Between Maggie and . . . well, everybody."

I could feel the pain in her voice, and I was sorry
for my part in making her unhappy. Pulling out
the chair beside her, I sat down. "I . . . I think I
understand, Carolyn."

She gave a small nod. "Sometimes I think it
would have been better if Sam and I had waited.
Not just better for Maggie, but for you, too. You've
had to make a lot of adjustments. It couldn't have
been easy leaving Washington at the beginning of
your senior year."

I nodded. "There've been a couple of adjustments," I said. But what I was thinking was, if Dad and Carolyn hadn't gotten married, if we hadn't moved here, *I would never have met Josh.* "But now I'm glad we came," I added awkwardly.

She glanced at me, surprised. "Do you really mean that, Lauren?"

I thought of the way Josh had kissed me on that old sofa, in the shadow of the plane he loved. I thought of my father's happiness, of Carolyn's bright smile at breakfast, and I realized that she really did give a lot of herself to Maggie and me. There was love here in our home, even if my family had changed.

"Yes, I mean it," I said.

Carolyn smiled as she reached out to pick up a yellow mum that was lying on the table. "I just want us to be friends."

Friends? A few weeks ago I would have said that wasn't possible. But a few weeks ago I hadn't known what love was. I hadn't known what it was like to feel somebody else's pain. Now I did. Josh was teaching me, and so was Annie. And Carolyn.

"Okay," I said with a smile. "Friends."

Carolyn leaned back in her chair with a little laugh. "Well, one friend to another, Lauren, I still think maybe it would have been better if your father and I had waited. Another year or two—it couldn't have made that much difference." She glanced at me. "Has Sam told you much about us?"

I shook my head. He'd tried to tell me, but I'd shut him out. I didn't want to hear about the woman he had loved before he ever met my mother.

"Sam and I were in love years ago, back in high

school," Carolyn told me. "I thought it was for keeps, and he did, too. When he gave me his class ring, it was like an engagement ring. That's why I didn't worry when he went away to college, even though I couldn't go with him."

"You couldn't?" I asked. "Why not?"

"Because my dad needed me to help out at home. My mom had died the year before, and I had a younger brother and sister. One was thirteen, the other ten. So, going away to college was pretty much out of the picture."

"What happened?"

"Sam met your mother and fell in love," she said matter-of-factly. "At Christmas he came home and told me that he'd found somebody else. He showed me her picture. She was tall and dark and very beautiful—like you." She looked down at the wedding band on her left hand. "I gave him back his class ring. After a while I heard that they were married."

I was silent for a moment, engulfed with sympathy for Carolyn and what she had gone through. "How . . . how did you feel when he told you?" I asked. I was thinking about Annie.

"I felt that I had nothing left to live for," she said quietly. "I cried for a long time. But after I calmed down and could look at it rationally, I realized that Sam had a right to choose for himself. He had a right to be happy."

"Even though it made you unhappy?"

"Yes, even though it made me unhappy. Because being unhappy meant I had to figure out what I really *did* want to do with my life. I tried a few different things. I was a secretary in Springfield at one point, but I found out that offices just aren't for me. Eventually I enrolled in the horticulture program at the junior college. That was where I met Bruce, in one of my classes. The marriage didn't work out, but after the divorce I still had Maggie. She was the best part. Then Sam and I ran into each other when I was visiting D.C., and we fell in love all over again. When your Dad said he wanted to move back to Vermilion so we could be married, it was the happiest day of my life." Her smile became self-conscious. "There you have it— the complete story."

"Falling in love with Dad," I said, "what was it like?"

She looked at me. Her eyes were misty and bright, as if she were remembering secret joys, and her voice was firm when she answered. "It was wonderful. I don't know how to explain to you how wonderful it felt. And there was absolutely nothing in the world that either of us could do to change the way we felt about each other."

I remembered the incredible way I had felt with Josh that night at the skating rink. It was the same feeling that Carolyn was describing. There was absolutely nothing in the world that I could do to change the way I felt about Josh. Now I understood why Dad and Carolyn couldn't have waited for another year. It was the same reason Josh and I couldn't wait.

Carolyn had been fingering the mum as she talked. Then she tucked the yellow blossom into the bowl on the table. "You know," she said thoughtfully, "I'm glad you asked me that question, Lauren. I've been so worried about Maggie that sometimes I lose perspective. I forget about us— about Sam and me, I mean."

She let out a sigh. "Maggie will live through her unhappiness. But Sam and I are right for each other, right now."

"Does that mean you've decided about Maggie?" I asked.

"Yes," Carolyn said. "Maggie isn't going to Springfield. She's staying here, with us. With her family." She gave me a lopsided grin. "We're not defunct yet! And I'm definitely going to stop thinking that maybe Sam and I should have postponed getting married."

"That sounds like a good idea," I said. "Love can't be postponed, can it?" I put my arms around her and we hugged. I might have started to cry if the doorbell hadn't rung.

It was Annie.

"I got it!" she cried. "I found the perfect dress! You're going to love it."

"That's great," I said. I held the door open. "Come in and show it to me."

Upstairs she pulled off her jeans and top and wriggled into the new dress. It was a shimmering emerald-green satin, exactly the color of her eyes. The off-the-shoulder bodice fit her snugly, and the skirt clung to her hips, before falling in shiny folds to her calves. A wide satin sash cinched her small waist.

"Wow! It's perfect on you!"

Annie turned in front of the mirror, fluffing up

her short, coppery hair. "Do you think Josh will like it?"

"Yes," I said. I sat down on the bed, suddenly serious, and pulled my knees under my chin. "Annie, Carolyn just told me an interesting story."

"She did?" Annie asked. "What kind of story?" She was retying the sash. "Do you think it looks better this way, or the way I had it before?"

"The way you had it before," I replied. "She told me about what happened when my dad met my mom and broke off their engagement."

"I didn't know they were ever engaged," she said, looking at me in the mirror. "What kind of jewelry do you think I ought to wear?"

"I don't know. Have you got some pearls?" I asked. "They weren't engaged, exactly. He'd given her his class ring, though."

"Back in those days," Annie said thoughtfully, "I guess that was as good as being engaged. She must have felt pretty awful when they broke up."

"She thought her life was over, that she had nothing to live for. But then she decided that he had a right to choose. He had a right to be happy, even if it made her unhappy."

Annie let her breath out between her teeth. "She's one woman in a thousand, if you ask me. Most people wouldn't feel that generous about it."

"But she said that being unhappy was *good* for her," I said. "It made her think about what she wanted to do with her life—other than be Dad's wife, I mean. She said she learned a lot."

Annie looked at herself in the mirror. "It's hard to imagine that being so unhappy could be good for you," she said, smoothing the green satin skirt, "no matter how much you learned." She turned her head to one side, examining herself critically. "I've got some pearls, but I don't think they're exactly right." Twisting around to face me, she asked, "Would you toss me the brush out of my purse, Lauren? The trouble with short hair is that you don't have a lot of options. Forward or back or to the side, that's all."

I fished in her purse and found her brush. "What would you do, say, if Josh got involved with somebody else?" I asked the question casually, but my insides were wound tight. "Would you take it the way Carolyn did?"

Annie brushed her hair back, away from her face. She stared at her reflection for a long time before answering, and I wondered what she was thinking. "I don't know," she said slowly. "I mean, I hope I would. You have to be adult about things like that. Love and jealousy and stuff, I mean. There's no point in crying gallons of tears about something you can't change."

"Annie, I—" I began.

Her gaze in the mirror shifted to me. "But of course," she said quickly, "that would never happen. Josh and I are in love, and nothing's going to change that, ever." She flipped her hair forward again with the brush. "Which way do you like it best? Forward or back?"

I sighed. I just couldn't bear to ruin her good mood. "Forward, I guess." I propped my chin on my knees and watched as Annie tried brushing her hair first to one side, then the other.

11

DAVID CALLED ON SUNDAY AFTERNOON, INVITING ME to go out for pizza with him that night. I said yes, knowing that that night I had to tell him I couldn't see him anymore. I still hadn't thought of a good reason, but I hoped he'd just accept what I told him, and I wouldn't have to make up an excuse.

We went to a new restaurant that had just opened up over on the Dixie Highway, called PizzaBurger.

I had never been there before, but I liked the place right away. The tables were covered with red-checked cloths, and a jungle of shiny green plastic foliage hung from the ceiling. There was an old jukebox in the corner and a blinking beer sign over the counter. I thought for an instant of the French restaurant back in Washington where Dad and I often ate on Sunday evenings. André, the headwaiter, would have snickered if he could have seen the plastic flowers and the paper napkin dispensers on the tables.

A group of kids from school were there when we came in, and David and I stopped at their booth to say hi before we sat down. It made me nervous to think that they might overhear what I had to say to David. I was relieved when they left, just before the waitress brought us our pizza.

We ate in silence for a minute. I knew I had to tell him right away before I lost my courage. But none of the opening lines I'd rehearsed that afternoon seemed right. *Listen, David, I've decided that I don't want to go out with you anymore. David, I need your opinion about something very important.*

And then I didn't have time to consider any more possibilities, because David was asking me to go with him to the Harvest Festival.

"I know it's still a few weeks away," he was saying, "but it's sort of a big deal here, and I thought I'd ask you early."

I put down my fork. "Uh, David," I said, "I . . . I—"

He grinned at me. "You've got cheese on your chin." As I reached for my napkin, he added, "Listen, it's okay. On you, cheese looks cute."

"David," I said again, trying to make my voice sound firm, "I'm serious. I'm sorry, but I can't go to the Harvest Festival with you. In fact, I don't think we ought to go out again."

"What?" he asked, as if he weren't sure he'd heard right.

"I said," I repeated quietly, "that I can't go to the Harvest Festival. And I don't think we ought to date anymore."

"But ... but why not?" There was a look of stunned dismay on his face. "What's wrong? What's changed between us?"

"Nothing's wrong," I said. "Nothing's changed between us. You haven't done anything or said anything to make this happen. I just don't want to, that's all." I knew I sounded cold, but I was afraid if I tried to be any nicer, I wouldn't be able to go through with it.

"But I thought you ... I mean, I thought we were—" He floundered for a moment. "Just last week, you told Annie—"

"Annie misunderstood," I said. I pushed my pizza away. The restaurant seemed very warm, and my appetite had vanished. He wasn't going to make this easy. "She misunderstood. And I didn't have the ... I didn't have the courage to tell her she was wrong."

"What are you saying, Lauren?" He paused, his gaze searchingly on me. "You mean, you don't ... like me?"

"Not in the way you—not in that way," I said bleakly. "I'm sorry, David. I truly am."

He was still looking at me, and I could see the pain in his brown eyes. I looked away.

"I don't get it. I just don't get it," he muttered. "Everything between us was great. Terrific. And now all of a sudden—" When I looked back at him, I saw that his hurt look was mixed with growing anger. "There's somebody else, isn't there?"

It was more of a demand than a question, and it caught me off guard. "I—I, uh, no, of course there isn't," I stumbled.

But he'd read the truth in my eyes. "Yes, there is," he said, his voice gruff. "Don't make it worse by trying to lie to me, Lauren. Who is he?"

"There's nobody," I said. I'd been so naive, thinking that all I had to do was explain, and he would accept it! "Even if there were," I added defensively, "it's not fair to ask."

David scowled, and his jaw tightened. "You don't know very many people here yet," he said, half to himself. "It must be somebody you knew before, back in Washington. An old boyfriend maybe."

I hesitated. Maybe it would be better to let him think that it *was* somebody from back home.

I opened my mouth to agree with him, then snapped it shut again. I'd gotten myself into this situation in the first place by letting people think something that wasn't true. I wasn't going to make that mistake again. "No, David, you're wrong," I said firmly.

But he obviously hadn't been listening; he was still thinking out loud. "Maybe it isn't somebody from back home," he said. He looked at me, his eyes narrowing, the muscles in his neck taut. "You do know somebody here. You know Josh."

I sucked in my breath.

The light of realization came into his eyes. "It's Josh, isn't it?" he demanded, leaning forward.

"Of course not," I said, trying to sound indignant. "Josh and Annie are—"

"To hell with Josh and Annie," he said angrily. "It's you and Josh, isn't it? It was you and Josh, even while you were letting me think you cared about me!" His voice went up a notch. "That remark your kid sister made at the game—that stuff about Josh having two girlfriends. She knew the real story, didn't she?"

I stared at him, feeling panicked. He was furious, even angrier than I'd expected. Was this how Annie was going to react when she learned the truth?

"Excuse me," the waitress interrupted, coming up to our table. "Can I get you something else?"

"No," David snapped.

I pushed my half-eaten pizza toward her. I wasn't at all hungry anymore. "You can take this," I said. When she'd gone, I stood up. "David, I really don't want to talk about it anymore. You don't need to drive me home—I can walk."

"Wait," he said, grabbing my wrist. "Sorry," he muttered. "I guess I lost my temper for a minute."

I sat down. "You know," he said bitterly, releasing my wrist, "I guess it's better this way. At least I know now. I don't like being made a fool of, you know." He shook his head, then his eyes flashed at me. "What about Annie? Does she know yet?" he asked. "I can't believe you'd lie to your best friend. That you'd actually *cheat* on her with her boyfriend."

I felt as if he'd pushed a knife into my heart and twisted it. I wanted to get up again, to escape, but I couldn't. His eyes pinned me to my seat.

"And not just your best friend, but your cousin. Family. What did she ever do to you, Lauren? How did she ever deserve this?"

I could only stare at him dumbly. His voice was the voice of my own conscience.

"Haven't you thought about the way she's going

to feel when she finds out? And she's going to find out sooner or later. You can't keep something like this a secret in a town like Vermilion."

"I . . . we don't intend to keep it a secret."

"No, I don't suppose you do," he said. "When do you plan on telling her? Soon, I hope."

"I . . . don't know. It's complicated." My head was swimming. "David, please, do we have to keep talking about it?"

"If you don't tell her soon," he said, very quietly, "I'll tell her myself."

I stared at him. "But why should you get involved?" I asked. "What is it to you?"

"It's not right to string her along," he said. "She shouldn't find out accidentally. It would be better if she heard it from a . . . a *real* friend."

I knew what he was implying. And he was right. I *wasn't* a real friend. Suddenly I couldn't listen any longer, couldn't cope with any more complications. The restaurant was unbearably hot, and I felt as if I couldn't breathe.

"If you're going to tell her," I said evenly, "I guess you'll tell her, no matter what I say."

I was almost running when I left the Pizza-Burger. It wasn't quite dark yet, and the cool fall air was refreshing on my hot face. David's accusations had rocked me. It had been bad enough to hear my own conscience accusing me of betraying my best friend, but his confirming every little thing I'd ever done to hurt Annie—it was unbearable. He was right, too, about everything. I'd lied to Annie, I'd cheated on her and betrayed her trust. And not only in my thoughts but in my actions. I thought of how Josh and I had felt together, just the day before. It had seemed so beautiful, so wonderful, so right. Listening to Carolyn, I had understood just how right it was, and I had felt a ray of hope. I'd thought then that maybe there was a way out of the mess we were in.

But then, listening to David, I understood how *wrong* it was. We had been wrong to give in to our feelings for each other when we weren't free. Tears filled my eyes. What was right for the two of us was wrong for the three of us. There wasn't any way out, except . . .

I stopped dead in my tracks as it hit me. I hadn't been aware of anything but my own thoughts as I walked. But now I felt the black night around me and saw the maples and elms, dark, rustling, shadows against a dark sky. There *was* a way out. If I broke off with Josh before things went any further, Annie would never have to know what had happened between us. I pulled in my breath. Living without him would be torment. But it would be less painful than living with the knowledge of what I was doing to Annie.

When I got home, I went straight to the phone to call Josh. I couldn't tell him what I had decided over the phone—I had to do it face-to-face—but I could let him know that I'd broken off with David, and tell him that I needed desperately to talk with him. But I couldn't reach him. He and his dad were out at the airport, his mom told me, working on old Jenny. I thought of calling Annie to tell her that David and I had broken up, but I decided not to.

I'd have to give her a reason, and I was too tired, too upset, to try to conjure up any more explanations. Even though it was only a little after nine, I went to bed.

I had planned to tell Annie about David on Monday morning, but we didn't go to school together, the way we usually did. She was supposed to bring her computer to school to do some sort of demonstration at an all-day computer fair, and she had to be in the gym early to get ready. I had completely forgotten about it until I arrived at her house and her mom reminded me. That meant I wouldn't be able to see Josh, either. He was going to be in the fair, too, which meant that he wouldn't be in homeroom or any of his morning classes.

It was a miserable day for me. As it turned out, I didn't have to tell Annie, or Josh, or anybody about David and me, because by the end of the day, everybody knew. I suppose what started the gossip was the fact that we didn't eat lunch together for the first time since school started. David probably told one or two of his friends, too.

I might have been imagining it, but throughout the afternoon I thought there was more than the usual amount of gossip buzzing among the other kids, and a few times I thought I saw people glancing at me. It wasn't that I minded people knowing that David and I had broken up; in fact, that was almost a relief. What I really minded was not knowing if David had told anyone *why* we'd split up.

Annie caught me at my locker after school. "I

don't believe it!" she exclaimed. Her arms were full of computer printouts, which she dumped into her locker. "Is it really true, Lauren? Have you and David actually broken up?"

I was so nervous, my stomach hurt, and I couldn't bear to look her in the eyes. What if she knew? What if David had told her, the way he threatened to? Shaking like a leaf, I stuck my head into my locker and frantically rummaged around, although I had no idea what I was looking for. I tried to make my voice sound normal and offhand, but it came out sounding like a squeak from a rusty door hinge. "Uh, yeah. We did."

Annie pulled me around to face her. "Lauren Michaels, how come you didn't tell me about this? I mean, you're obviously upset about it."

"I—I didn't have a chance," I said nervously. "It just happened last night, and you've been at the computer fair all day."

She looked more concerned than hurt. Maybe David hadn't told her. I relaxed, but only a little; she was still pretty upset. "But you could have called me last night," Annie went on. "I mean, I thought we weren't going to have any secrets from each other. And here's this big thing going on in your life, and I didn't even know about it! I had to hear it from somebody else first."

I was silent, thinking of the other thing she didn't know.

She put her hand on my arm, misreading my silence. "I'm sorry, Lauren," she said gently. "I didn't mean to give you a hard time. I know you must be pretty upset about it. Was it your idea, or David's?"

"It—it was mutual, I guess."

"But I don't understand! Everything seemed just fine between you two on Friday night at the game. You looked like you were getting along great. What went wrong?"

My face was flaming red, and my hands were unsteady. I bent over to cram my dirty gym shorts into my book bag, hiding my red cheeks. "Nothing went wrong," I muttered. "It . . . it just wasn't right, that's all. Not for me anyway. Or for him, either."

"Well, I still don't understand," Annie said.

"We just called it quits, and that's all there is to it. Believe me."

My words sounded false in my own ears, and I guess Annie thought so, too, because her eyes widened, and she asked, "Is there somebody else?"

I was caught off balance. "Somebody . . . else?"

She made a quick, impatient, gesture. "You know, is he interested in another girl?" She frowned. "He dated Brenda Cohen for a couple of months last year, but I don't think he was really serious about her. Honest, Lauren, I wouldn't have encouraged you to go out with him if I'd thought he'd string you along and then dump you for another girl. That's a pretty dirty trick, if you ask me! Only a real jerk would do something that cruddy to somebody else."

"Annie, you're jumping to conclusions! Please stop!" I couldn't blame her for being angry, but she was directing it at the wrong person. It was *my* dirty trick that had started this whole thing. *I* was the jerk! She should be angry at me, not David. Now I knew, beyond the shadow of a doubt, that I was right to end it between Josh and me. And the sooner the better.

"But I don't see—"

I shook my head. "There's no other girl, Annie. David isn't a jerk. He wasn't stringing me along, and he didn't dump me. Period. The end."

Before she had time to answer, Josh came up. He was carrying a computer printer against one hip. "Hey, Annie," he said, "they're getting ready to lock up the gym. If you want to take your computer home, you'd better hurry up and get it."

"I will," Annie said. "Have you heard the news?"

Josh shifted the printer to the other hip. "What news?"

"About Lauren and David. They broke up."

Josh swung around to face me, his eyes sharply questioning. "So, you did it," he said softly.

I nodded.

"Hey," Annie said, looking from Josh to me, "did you know this was going to happen?"

Josh threw me a quick glance. "Uh, well . . ."

Annie put her hands on her hips, turning to me. "Did you tell Josh that you were going to break up with David?" Without waiting for an answer, she looked at Josh. "I wish you two would let me in on your little secrets."

Josh looked at me, but I gave an almost imperceptible shake of my head. He seemed about to speak anyway, but Annie slammed her locker shut and grabbed her book bag.

"Well, I don't have time to argue about it," she

said. "I don't want to leave my computer locked up in the gym all night." She took a few running steps backward. "Remember, no more secrets!" she called. Then she was gone.

"I was *this* close to telling her," Josh said, holding his thumb and his forefinger a hair apart.

"I know. I'm glad you didn't." My voice sounded shaky, and I took a deep breath. The main hall of Vermilion High wasn't exactly the most private place for a talk like this one, but maybe that was good. Maybe it was better that we weren't someplace where he could put his arms around me. If he did, I was sure my resolve would crumble.

"I've been thinking about this whole thing," I said miserably, "and I've come to a conclusion. There's only one way out of this mess, and that's for us to . . . to end our relationship." I swallowed the lump that had suddenly risen in my throat. "All these secrets . . . I feel as if I'm trapped in the middle of a huge, sticky, web, and I can't get out. I want to be with you all the time." My voice broke, but I forced myself to go on. "But after I leave you, I feel terrible about sneaking around. Every time I look at Annie, I feel like a total jerk. I can't bear the thought of hurting her, Josh. I can't go on seeing you. I'm sorry, but—" I blinked back the hot tears. "I'm sorry."

There. The words were out. I suddenly felt cold and bereft. I had betrayed Annie in the most awful way. Things would never be the same between us. I'd pushed David out of my life. My father was occupied with his new family, and I was living in a strange place, far from everything I knew. Worse yet, I would never again know the joy of being in Josh's arms, never be able to take the final step of actually making love with him.

Josh pushed his dark hair off his forehead. Two deep lines appeared on either side of his mouth.

"What happened on Saturday—" he said at last, "does that have anything to do with the way you're feeling?"

I nodded slowly, not looking at him. "Yes, in a way. Before Saturday everything was sort of . . . I don't know, sort of inside me, private. After—after Saturday everything was out in the open." I shut my eyes, remembering the way his hands had felt. "I'm not saying it was wrong, Josh, but David reminded me that we're not the only ones involved in this. After I talked to him, I knew that I couldn't hurt Annie this way."

"David?" Josh asked sharply. "What's he got to do with this?"

I looked up at him, feeling miserable. "David guessed. About us, I mean. He was pretty upset about the whole thing. He said some things . . . and he threatened to tell Annie."

Josh's face darkened. "I'll talk to him," he muttered. He gave me a long look. "If you want to break up with me, Lauren, that's up to you. But I said it before, and I'll say it again. I love you, and no matter what happens, I'll keep on loving you."

I nodded. I would love him, too. Knowing that we could never be together left a bitter taste in my mouth, but it was better than letting Annie know my secret. This way she would never have to know how I had betrayed her.

12

THE NEXT TWO WEEKS WERE AGONIZING. I PLAYED IT straight, with Annie and with myself. I stopped walking to homeroom and to English class with Josh. I ached to be with him, to talk with him, but I didn't even telephone him, and he didn't call me, either. He did stop me once in the cafeteria, to say that he'd talked to David and that he didn't think David would say anything to Annie. But that was all. When he walked away, I felt as if the last lifeline had been cut and I was alone. It was miserable.

I went through every day feeling as if I were in an isolation tank. I had made some friends in my classes, but I didn't feel like listening to them talk about their boyfriends, so I began to stay to myself. I didn't go out with other guys, either, even though Mitch asked me out several times.

The hardest thing was acting as if everything was okay when I was with Annie. After David and I broke up, she went out of her way to spend more time with me, and naturally, she had plenty of suggestions for dates.

"If you don't want to date Mitch," she said one evening as we sat in my room talking, "how about Jerry Erickson? He's a really nice guy. He and Ellen just broke up a couple of weeks ago." She threaded her needle with green thread, squinting. She'd decided that her Harvest Festival dress should be just a little shorter, and now, with one more week to go before the dance, she was hemming it.

"Thanks," I said, watching her take several stitches. "I think I'll pass."

I stretched out on my bed. I felt more comfortable with Annie now that I was no longer seeing Josh secretly, but I still didn't feel like the same girl who had shared everything with her.

Annie snipped off a thread. "Lauren, I need to ask you something." Her tone was serious. "Something important."

"Well, ask."

"Have you noticed Josh being . . . well, different, lately?"

"Different?" I tried to control my voice. "How do you mean?"

She waved the scissors vaguely. "Oh, I don't know. Distant, maybe. He doesn't always seem to connect with me, and we don't go out as often as we used to. Before, it was Friday and Saturday night and a couple of times during the week. Now, I only see him half that."

I cleared my throat. "Maybe he's busy. He's got some kind of air show coming up, doesn't he? He and his dad are probably working to get ready. And anyway, it's not summer anymore. Maybe he has to study during the week."

"Maybe," Annie conceded. "The Antique Air Show is on Saturday. But . . . he just doesn't seem the same, somehow. I can't quite put my finger on it." She gave a little laugh. "If I didn't know him so well, I might think he was seeing somebody else."

"Don't be silly," I said sharply.

"I guess I am being silly," she said, lifting her chin. "And I'm going to stop." She held up the dress against her. "What do you think? Is the length right?"

"Perfect," I said, but I wasn't looking at her dress. I was thinking about Josh. For an instant I wondered what would happen if he *did* break up with her. But I pushed the thought out of my mind as quickly as it appeared. I wasn't going to torment myself by thinking about possibilities that would never come to be.

Annie was still looking at the dress. "I still haven't decided on the jewelry," she said. "Pearls just don't seem right somehow."

Suddenly I had an idea. "I've got just the thing," I said. Taking a little white box out of the dresser drawer, I opened it, and showed her Mother's emerald pendant. "What would you think of borrowing this for the dance?"

The stone was a deep, true, green, the exact color of her dress. "Oh, Lauren, it's perfect!"

"It was my mother's. It's always been my favorite thing."

Annie's eyes shone. "I know it must mean a

great deal to you," she said softly. "I can't thank you enough, Lauren. But I'd feel better if you kept it for me until the dance."

Very carefully I put the pendant back in its box. I'd vowed that nobody else but me would ever wear it. But Annie's eyes were green, and her dress was green, and it was only for one night. It was the least I could do. "I'll bring it over when you're getting ready," I told her.

She nodded. "Listen, you don't have any plans for Saturday, do you? There's something I'd like to do."

"What is it?" I asked. "Does it involve a guy?"

"No," she said. "Just Josh."

I stared at her. This was too much. "And Josh is not a guy?"

"It's the air show," she said, ignoring my question. "You know, the one where Josh and his dad are going to race that old plane they've fixed up. They're taking off on Saturday morning, and they'll be back about five. I thought you and I could watch them take off. Then we could drive to Springfield to pick up the shoes I'm having dyed and be back by the time they land. How about it?"

I considered. Josh had spoken so affectionately of the old plane. I really wanted to see him fly it, and it was exciting to think that perhaps I might even see him win the race. Maybe it wasn't a very smart thing to do, but I could stay in the background, and after they landed, I could disappear.

"I'll tell you what," I said. "I'll go with you if I don't have to hang around afterward."

"Okay. You can drive my car home, if that's what you want," Annie said. "I'll ride home with Josh."

It was settled.

Saturday dawned clear and beautiful. Annie picked me up at eight and we drove to the airport. The parking lot was crowded with cars, and the concrete apron was filled with airplanes, dozens of them, most of them dating from the 1930s and 1940s.

Josh and his dad had rolled the biplane out of the hangar and were working on the engine. We waved, and Josh waved back. I was glad that he'd seen me, even though we couldn't talk. At least he'd know I still cared enough to want to share a proud day with him.

It looked as if the race was about to start. Annie had told me that it was a timed race, which meant the planes were handicapped and were flying a specified course against the clock.

In a few minutes the first plane took off, then a few minutes later, another. Josh's father climbed into the back cockpit of the biplane and gave a thumbs-up signal. Josh pushed the propeller around a couple of times, and the engine coughed, belching gray smoke. Then, with one last wave, he climbed into the front cockpit, and we watched the Jenny roll into line, her tail dragging. At last it was their turn. The plane, looking flimsy and frail, started down the grassy strip beside the runway.

"But they've missed the runway!" Annie cried, clutching my arm.

"The Jenny's designed to take off on grass," I said.

Annie looked at me. "How did you know that?"

"I . . . read it somewhere, I guess," I stammered. How could I have made such a dumb slip?

Annie was watching the plane, her eyes shaded. I watched, too, my heart pounding. The Jenny was one of the oldest planes of the show—over seventy years old! Would she really fly?

A little farther down the green strip of grass the old plane suddenly leapt into the air, feather-light, as if it had been boosted by an unseen hand. There was a long "ooh" from the watching crowd and enthusiastic applause. Its engine strong and steady, the Jenny climbed higher and higher, circling until it was only a tiny speck heading west in the bright sky above. I could imagine Josh in the cockpit, his dark hair falling over his forehead, his eyes on the distant horizon, already plotting their triangular course west to the Mississippi, then north into Wisconsin, then southeast and back to Vermilion.

Annie gave a sigh of satisfaction and reached for her car keys. "Well, they're off. Ready to go to Springfield?"

Our shopping trip was uneventful. Annie's newly dyed shoes were a perfect match for her green dress, and she bought a small silver handbag. We had a late lunch at a natural food restaurant. The food was good, but it was hard for me to concentrate either on what I was eating or on our conversation. I tried to relax and have a good time with Annie, the way I used to, but I guess I was feeling preoccupied. I kept thinking of Josh, somewhere high over the empty prairie, in that frail plane built of cloth and wire and wood.

After lunch we started back. The race had been planned so that all the planes would return to Vermilion before dark. But as we drove back from Springfield, I noticed that the weather was changing rapidly. Thunderheads were piled high in the sky behind us, replacing the clear blue and stretching in a heavy, ominous, line all along the western horizon. As gusts of wind buffeted Annie's Volkswagen, I began to feel a rising uneasiness. Would Josh and his father have to change course because of the weather? My hands felt clammy as I looked back over my shoulder at the looming clouds. There was a sinking feeling in the pit of my stomach. Was Josh in danger?

When we reached the airport, I saw a crowd of spectators clustered along the fence and on the apron. Everyone seemed to be keeping an eye on the threatening clouds and watching the planes come in one at a time. As each one landed, a cheer went up, somebody would chalk some numbers on a big scoreboard, and people would rush out to take pictures. On the board I spotted Josh's name and his dad's, together with their plane, the Curtiss JN-4. The landing time was still blank.

Annie kept looking at her watch. Off to the west a spear of lightning stabbed the ground, and thunder growled, causing us both to jump.

The plane that had taken off just before Josh's plane came in for a landing. Now there were only five planes out.

"Any minute now," Annie said, but she didn't sound convinced.

My mouth was beginning to feel very dry. "Maybe—" I cleared my throat and tried again. "Maybe they had to go around the storm." I looked up. Another plane had appeared in the darkening sky. Lightning flickered from cloud to cloud. Thunder rumbled around us. "Maybe that's them!"

But it wasn't. It was the plane that had taken off last. I was trying not to think of what might have happened to the small plane, but every second we waited seemed to stretch out forever, and my mind filled with terrible pictures.

The man at the board chalked up some more numbers. There were only two planes left now.

"That settles it," Annie said, looking at the board. "Let's go to the terminal building and find out what's going on."

Inside the terminal Jumbo was sitting behind the counter at the radio, scanning the sky through the window and munching on a sandwich. There were some other people in front of the counter, but Annie made her way through. I hung back, clenching my hands into tight fists. I didn't know how I would do it, but I had to try to keep my anxiety from showing, so that Annie wouldn't see how much I cared about Josh. I'd always been a strong person, but then my knees felt rubbery. I was sick with worry and shaking with the effort it took to keep my feelings to myself. Outside, there was a flash and a crash of thunder. The storm was very close now, almost upon us.

"Jumbo, do you know where they are?" I heard Annie ask. "Have they checked in?"

Suddenly the radio interrupted. "Corsair F-25 to base."

Jumbo flicked a switch. "Base here, over."

"Did you copy the distress call from Curtiss JN-4?"

There was a stir in the crowd.

"Negative, Corsair," Jumbo said, his voice flat. "What have you got?"

"Their transmission was breaking up, but I caught a piece of it. They've got an electrical problem, and the storm's closing in on them. They're looking for someplace to put her down."

There was a sudden silence in the terminal lobby. Everyone was listening to Jumbo and to the crackling, faraway voice on the radio.

"You mean, they've got to make an emergency landing?" Annie asked, in a shaking voice.

An emergency landing? A choking fear rose in my throat. All the memories of the past few weeks flooded me. I remembered Josh's hands on my shoulders, his fingers on my face, his lips on mine, his voice saying, "I love you, Lauren." I couldn't hold on any longer.

"Josh!" I heard myself cry. "No!"

13

I WAS DIMLY AWARE OF A BABBLE OF CONFUSION around me. Voices were saying things I didn't understand, and somebody was helping me into a seat. Then Annie was a blur in front of me, with a cup of water in her hands, and Jumbo's nasal voice floated toward me from a distance, "Slap her—that's what you're supposed to do when somebody's hysterical."

But Annie didn't slap me. Her green eyes were wide, and she was staring at me with growing comprehension. It was the sight of her face, more than anything else, that made me regain control. I shuddered, gulped down a last sob, and pulled myself up straight.

"I'm sorry," I said. I could feel my shoulders shaking, hear my voice crack. The room was unbearably cold. "I didn't mean to—"

Annie pushed the cup of water at me. "Don't say anything. Here. Drink this."

I drank it, shivering. Somebody took the empty

cup. The other people drifted away, and Annie and I were left alone. I had never seen her look like this before. Her face was very pale, her mouth set in a firm, hard, line. Her green eyes were cold and brittle as green glass.

I knew I had given away my secret. She probably hated me now. But I couldn't think about that. I couldn't think about anything except finding out that Josh was safe. I huddled miserably in the chair and wrapped my arms around myself.

Annie went to the window. For a long time she stood there, her shoulders hunched, and then she came to sit down beside me. There were traces of tears on her cheeks.

"There's nothing to do but wait until we hear something," she said tonelessly.

We waited in silence while the minutes ticked slowly past. Ten minutes, fifteen, twenty. I was conscious of Annie sitting tensely beside me, conscious of people leaning against the concrete-block walls, sitting on windowsills, not talking; conscious of Jumbo, for once without something to eat, just holding the mike in his big fist, waiting. But above all, I was conscious that I might never again see Josh, and there was an icy emptiness inside me.

The telephone's shrill ring startled everyone. Jumbo reached for it, spoke into it. Then a grin split his face, and he jabbed his thumb into the air in a quick, triumphant, gesture.

"They're down safe!" somebody said, and somebody else clapped. I let out my breath with an explosive sigh. Josh was safe! He was *safe*! All around us people were slapping one another on the back, hugging and laughing.

But Annie and I didn't hug. Jumbo called her, and she walked stiffly to the phone. A few minutes later she came back.

"It was Josh's dad," she said. "He was calling from a farmhouse a mile or so from where they put the plane down. They're both fine. But they need some tools and equipment." She looked at me. "I volunteered to take them to him. You'd better come, too. It'll take an hour to get there."

I nodded and stood up unsteadily. I didn't want to ride with her. But I had to see for myself that Josh was all right. I followed her and a couple of guys to the hangar, and we put some tools and things into a big box and lugged it to the Volkswagen. Then Annie and I got in and drove off.

The storm had passed over us on its way eastward, taking with it the thunder and lightning, and the sky was now a dirty gray, darkening into dusk. It was still raining lightly, and we rode in silence except for the splat of the windshield wipers. Then Annie turned to me.

"Are you going to tell me about it?" she asked. Her knuckles were white on the steering wheel.

"I'm not sure what to say," I whispered. It was true. Where could I begin?

"You're in love with him, aren't you?"

I cleared my throat and shook myself. Being so afraid for Josh—thinking that maybe he'd even died—had put everything in perspective. It was time for the truth, past time. It had been, all along.

"Yes," I said.

"And he's in love with you?"

"I . . . I—"

"No more lies," she cried.

"Yes, he is," I said.

There was a long silence. Then she asked, "How long has this been going on? This sneaking around, I mean."

"We haven't been sneaking around."

"Have you seen him? Other than at school, or with me, I mean."

I couldn't deny it. "Yes." The word was only a whisper.

"Alone?"

"Yes."

"You can call it what you like," she said flatly, her eyes on the road. "In my book it's called sneaking around. I thought you were too honest for something like that, Lauren."

I turned to her, my hands out, pleading. "We didn't mean for it to happen, Annie. It wasn't something that either of us planned."

She let out her breath in an impatient rush. "I don't believe you," she said. "I think that you decided from the beginning that you wanted my boyfriend. So you went after him. And you took him." There was a harsh, bitter, edge to her words. "I can't believe that I thought you were my friend, that I trusted you. You *stole* him."

"It's not true!" I said, clenching my hands. "It isn't."

"It must be, Lauren, or you would have come right out and told me the truth weeks ago."

"Josh was . . . we were going to tell you . . . after

his birthday party. We wanted to do it earlier, but there was the Harvest Festival and—"

She gave a sarcastic laugh. "And you thought you'd wait and make a fool of me for a bit longer, is that it?"

"No," I whispered, "that isn't it at all."

Annie gave me a hard look. "I don't believe you." Her mouth tightened, and she didn't speak another word for the rest of the drive.

Josh and his father had landed the biplane on a graveled farm road between two fields of corn, and they were already at work on the engine when we drove up. Josh's dad gave us a wave, and Josh stepped around the plane to meet us. His dark hair was slick with rain, and his blue shirt was plastered to his shoulders and chest. He grinned at us, but I guess when he saw Annie's set face and my pale one, he must have realized something was wrong. His grin faded, and when he looked at me again, there was a question in his eyes.

I stepped forward. At least, now that the truth was out, we wouldn't have to pretend. "You're okay?" I asked, searching his face. "You're not hurt?"

"Not a scratch," Josh said. "We had a few uneasy moments when the storm hit, but Jenny came down light as a feather. She's got so much lift that she can land almost anywhere." He paused and looked back at the plane. "We've tracked the problem to the electrical system. The magneto went out. That's what generates the spark."

"Have you got it fixed yet?" Annie's tone was chilly.

"No. We needed the tools you brought, and now Dad says we have to have the spare magneto that's in the hangar." He went around the car and took out the box we'd brought. "I'll ride to the airport with you, get what we need, and bring it back in my truck."

Annie got back in the car. "Well, come on, then," she said abruptly.

If it hadn't been for Josh, the drive back would have been even worse than the drive out. There was silence for a few minutes while Annie negotiated the blind turns on the gravel road with typical, hair-raising, speed. When we got onto the highway, Josh said, "Well, I suppose you know now, Annie."

"You suppose right," she said, keeping her eyes forward. "Lauren gave it away when we heard you'd crash-landed."

"I don't know what to say," Josh said. "I know *sorry* isn't enough. But I *am* sorry." He hesitated, glancing at her. "Please don't be angry at Lauren," he added. "*I'm* the one you should be angry with. I let you down."

"But you didn't let me down the way Lauren did," Annie said flatly. "Lauren was my best friend."

Josh stepped in to defend me. "But Lauren didn't—"

Annie interrupted him angrily. "You're no better than she is, Josh. You should have had the courage to come out and tell me the truth in the first place.

Sure, it would have been hard for me to accept, but I would have got over it eventually. But for Lauren to go behind my back! I trusted her! And she . . . betrayed me. I'll never be able to trust her again, ever."

Hot tears slid down my cheeks. Everything that Annie said was true. I had been her best friend. We'd shared our deepest, most intimate, secrets. She'd always been ready to listen, ready to help when I needed her. And I'd repaid her friendship and trust by being disloyal. Whether I had meant to or not didn't matter. The point was that I had betrayed her.

It was nearly nine by the time Annie let me out in front of my house. I said good-night, but she didn't answer; she just put the Volkswagen in gear and drove off. I was so wrung out that I wanted to go straight to my room, but Dad stopped me on the stairs.

"We're having a family talk, honey," he said. "Would you mind joining us for a few minutes?" He saw the reluctance on my face and added, "You look tired. I wouldn't ask you if it weren't important."

With a sigh I followed him into the kitchen. I hoped this wasn't going to be anything melodramatic. I'd had enough crises for one day.

Carolyn was there, and Maggie. They all had mugs of mint tea, and Carolyn poured one for me as I sat down at the table. I wondered whether I should tell them what had happened with Josh's plane, but I decided not to. I didn't want to worry them. It looked as though they had problems of their own.

"We've been talking about things here at home," Dad said. "We've come to a conclusion."

"We've decided I'm right," Maggie put in smugly. "About being a defunct family."

"Dysfunctional, dear," Carolyn corrected automatically, then smiled. "After you and I talked, Lauren, I told Maggie that it wasn't a good idea for her to go live in Springfield. From her reaction, I realized that we weren't going to be able to handle this ourselves."

I looked at her, wondering what she was getting at.

"When you're in the middle of an emotional situation," Dad added, "sometimes it's kind of hard to see what's involved. It's easy to lose your bearings, lose your perspective."

I nodded. I knew about that, all right.

"So I talked to a therapist, Dr. Robbins, at the Family Clinic here in town," Carolyn went on. "She's willing to meet with us." She glanced at me. "But she says that we all need to see her, Lauren, because our problems are family problems."

"But I'm not involved," I protested. Maggie was Dad and Carolyn's problem, not mine.

Dad looked at me. "Are you a part of this family?"

Was I a part of this family?

I looked around. I had lost Annie, my best friend, my cousin, my almost-sister. I didn't want to lose Dad, or Carolyn—or even Maggie.

"When's our appointment?" I asked.

* * *

I don't know how I got through the rest of the weekend. It wasn't easy. I tried to call Annie on Sunday, but she wasn't home, and Aunt Ruth said she wouldn't be back until late in the evening. Hesitantly she asked me if Annie and I had quarreled. I wasn't sure what to say, but it seemed best to tell the truth. So, I said yes, simply, and let it go at that. I left a message, but Annie didn't return my call. I wasn't surprised.

That night Josh came over. We sat on the porch swing, watching the moon come up over the maple trees. The storm had blown the leaves away, and the branches were bare against the bright moon. We didn't talk much. I guess we were both busy with our own thoughts. But it was a comfort to be with him.

Finally he turned to me, and slid his arm across the back of the wooden swing. "I haven't stopped loving you," he said quietly. "Now that Annie knows, I want us to be together."

It was as simple as that. It had been simple all along. I was the one who had made it complicated.

"I want that, too," I whispered.

He put his fingers on my cheek and turned my face to him. His face was dark in the moonlight, but I could see the love shining in his eyes. I could feel it in his kiss, too. But when I kissed him back, I kept seeing Annie's taut face, hearing the bitterness in her voice, and I felt a deep, unbearable, sadness.

Josh seemed to understand, and he didn't press me. Pulling away gently, he cradled my head against his shoulder and stroked my hair as we rocked on the swing.

Later, when he was ready to leave, he asked, "Do you want to go to the Harvest Festival dance Friday night?"

I shook my head. I knew how Annie would feel seeing Josh and me together. I wouldn't be able to watch her take her place in the Queen's Court, or even as the queen, without breaking down.

"Well, I'll think of something else for that night," Josh said. "Hang in there, Lauren. I know it's not easy just now, but the hurt will pass."

I wished I could believe him.

Because Annie's locker was next to mine, we couldn't avoid seeing each other. But she never said a word to me. She kept her face turned away so she didn't have to look at me, either. I felt terrible about it. Even being with Josh didn't make me feel much better.

The whole week passed in a horrible, painful, blur. On Thursday afternoon, Dad, Carolyn, Maggie, and I had our first session with Dr. Robbins. It started off uneasily, but by the time it was over, I think we all felt better. Somehow, talking to one another seemed a little easier with the therapist there. Maybe we could work things out after all. Afterward, at home, I went into the kitchen to help Carolyn, and I found myself telling her everything that had happened with Annie and Josh. The words gushed out, and I started crying as I told her.

With a sympathetic sigh she put her arms around

me. "What a difficult time you've had," she said softly, smoothing my hair.

"I've made it difficult for myself," I said, in a muffled voice.

Carolyn stepped back, looking at me. "Have you talked to Annie in the last few days?"

I shook my head. "She won't say anything to me. I see her at school, but she looks the other way."

"Maybe you should go to her house," she suggested. "I know that she's feeling very hurt. But your friendship is important to both of you."

"I don't know," I said doubtfully. "She might be so angry that she'd slam the door in my face."

Carolyn raised her eyebrows. "But then again, maybe she won't. Anyway, what have you got to lose by trying?"

I sighed. "I'll think about it."

On Friday, Annie was elected queen of the Harvest Festival. The balloting took place during the lunch hour, and by the last period the votes were all counted, and the queen and her court were introduced at an all-school assembly. I had told Josh I didn't think we ought to sit together, and I'd found a seat by myself in the third row. When Annie was introduced as the queen, I could see the pride and pleasure on her face. But there was pain, too, in the lines of her mouth, and I could see tears glinting on her cheeks. Tears had sprung to my eyes, as well, and as I stood with the other students to applaud, I had to blink them away. I loved Josh, but I loved Annie, too. How could I ever live with the pain I had caused her?

By that evening I'd made up my mind. I told Carolyn I wouldn't be home for dinner. Borrowing Dad's car, I drove straight over to Annie's house. My heart was pounding when I rang the bell.

Aunt Ruth answered the door. Giving me a quick hug, she said, "I'm glad you've come. Annie's in her room, getting ready. She's got to be at the football field to get on the float at seven-fifteen."

"I won't be long," I assured her. I went up the stairs and knocked on Annie's door. "It's me."

Silence. Then there was a satiny rustle. "Come in," Annie said.

Very slowly I opened the door.

Annie was standing in front of the mirror. When she turned to face me, I gasped. I had never seen her look so beautiful. The emerald-green dress matched the green of her eyes and hugged her body perfectly. Her coppery hair was brushed to a burnished shine, and her face was rosy.

"Annie, you look—" I stopped. "I can't think of the words."

"Try the dictionary," she said. There was a wry twist to her mouth.

"—stunning," I finished.

"That's not very original." She wasn't looking at me, but there was a little of the old Annie in her voice.

"It's the best I can do," I said. "Annie, I . . . I came to congratulate you. On being selected queen, I mean."

"Thanks." Her tone was flat. I couldn't read the look in her eyes.

"And to bring you this," I added. I held out a

small white box. It was the necklace I'd promised to lend her, my mother's emerald pendant.

All she said was, "Oh, Lauren," but I could see the tears building in her eyes, and I started to cry, too.

She turned so I could fasten the necklace around her neck. My fingers were shaking. "My mother told me people with green eyes should always wear emeralds," I said. I tried to keep my voice steady. "I also came to apologize," I added softly. "I know that I should have told you how I felt about Josh at the very beginning, and I'm really sorry. But what I'm sorriest about is what I've done to our friendship. I know things will never be the same between us."

"I guess you're right," Annie said, but her tone was more resigned than bitter. "I don't think we can ever go back to the way we were, before this all happened."

I didn't know what else to say, so I turned to go, feeling the burden of sadness settle on my shoulders again. "Well," I said, "congratulations. You'll make a beautiful queen."

Annie put her hand on my arm. "Wait, Lauren. Just because we can't go back to the way we were, doesn't mean we can't have something." With a rustle of green satin, she sat down on the bed and picked up Baxter, holding him in her lap.

"I've been thinking all week, and I've realized that I can't force Josh to love me if you're the one he cares for. I also realized that things probably weren't as perfect between Josh and me as I thought. From the very beginning, I wanted more out of our relationship than he did. Looking back, I can see that." She drew herself up, and I was struck again by how beautiful she looked. "Anyway, soon we'll be graduating, doing different things. Josh and I would probably only have stayed together a little while longer."

I sat down beside her on the bed. "Do you mean—"

She cleared her throat. "I'm saying that losing Josh hurts. It hurts like hell, and I'm not going to try to hide it from you or from him. But losing you is worse, Lauren. You and I could have had a friendship that would go on for the rest of our lives." She looked down at Baxter and touched his ear with one finger. "I don't know what's left for us. Maybe nothing. Maybe something." She cleared her throat, and her lips curved in a sad smile. "Just don't ask me to double-date with you two."

There was a tap on the door. "Annie, it's quarter to seven," Aunt Ruth called.

Annie stood up and put Baxter on the pillow. Turning to face me, she said, "I have to go, Lauren."

I nodded. "Good-bye," I said, "and good luck."

She picked up her purse and went to the door. She turned, as if she were about to say something. But she just looked at me for a long moment and then left.

I sat down on the bed and picked up Baxter and cried.

"Where are we going?" I asked Josh, as he turned onto the highway. I had rushed home from

Annie's and changed into a dress. When Josh came to pick me up at seven-thirty, wearing slacks and a sports jacket, I was ready.

"Don't ask questions," he told me, laughing. Then, more soberly, he added, "You look as if you have something on your mind."

I told him what had happened at Annie's.

"Do you feel better now that you've talked to her?" he asked.

"A little." I felt tears prickling my eyelids. "But mostly I feel as if I've lost something really important, and I'll never have anything like it again."

My hand was on the seat between us, and Josh picked it up and kissed it. "Maybe you won't," he said. "I guess that's part of growing up. Losing things we can't replace and learning to live without them." We drove in silence, and after a while he turned into the airport and pulled up on the concrete apron, parking near the Cessna.

"Josh, what are we doing here?" I demanded.

"Going for a ride," Josh said innocently as we got out of the truck.

"But it's almost dark already!"

"So what? There's no rule that keeps you out of the sky after dark. It's a great time to fly." He opened the door to the plane. "No arguments. Get in."

I got in, Josh started the plane, and we taxied to the end of the runway. As we took off, the evening twilight was darkening the Illinois prairie, turning the fields and woods into a dusky, smoky, blue. Lights were blinking on everywhere, strings and clusters of them. We headed westward, and after a while I saw the lights of Springfield on the horizon. Josh got on the radio, and fifteen minutes later we were landing at Capital Airport.

"It's not Washington," Josh said, settling his arm around my shoulder, "and the food here isn't all that special. But there's a restaurant I like, a little Italian place. They're saving a table for us." He looked at me. "Do you like Italian food?"

"What if I said I didn't?"

Josh chuckled. "Well, there's a Chinese restaurant. But if you don't like Chinese, we're out of luck." His chuckle deepened into a laugh. "I guess we'd have to fly to Chicago. Or settle for pizza."

I leaned back, feeling Josh's arm warm and strong around me. I wasn't in Washington anymore. I'd lost that, for now anyway, and the life that went with it. I no longer had my father all to myself, but now I had a new family. And even though I'd lost Annie and our old, easy, closeness, I had gained Josh and a new and different kind of love.

Life was full of losses and gains, and I knew these wouldn't be the only ones in my life. Life was full of changes, too, and I had changed a lot since coming to Vermilion. I knew how much I had learned and grown in the past few months. And suddenly I was filled with hope, because I knew I was going to keep on learning and growing every place I went. This was only the beginning.

I turned to Josh with a huge smile on my face. He leaned over, wrapped his arms around me, and met the smile on my lips with his own.

About the Author

SUSAN BLAKE has written over fifty books for children and young adults, alone or with her husband, Bill Albert. She grew up on a small farm in Illinois, in a town not unlike the fictional one in *Stealing Josh*. She and her husband now live in the Texas hill country outside of Austin, where she enjoys gardening, studying wildlife, and reading. She has three children, three grandchildren, two cats, and four geese.